The Life's Too Short
Literary Review 01
New Writing From Pakistan

Edited by Faiza S. Khan and Aysha Raja

hachette
INDIA

First published in 2010 by Siren Publications, Pakistan
www.lifestooshort.pk
Publisher: Aysha Raja
Editor: Faiza S. Khan
Design: Atiq Uddin Ahmed, Design Red Communications

First published in India in a slightly altered form in 2011 by Hachette India
An Hachette UK company
www.hachetteindia.com

SRD

ISBN 978-93-5009-283-5

Hachette India
612/614 (6th Floor), Time Tower, M.G. Road,
Sector 28, Gurgaon - 122001, India

Typeset in Zapf Humanist 11/13
by InoSoft Systems

Printed and bound in India by
Manipal Technologies Limited, Manipal

MIX
Paper from
responsible sources
FSC™ C043100

contents

Editors' Note

This publication came about as an exercise in curiosity. While Pakistani fiction in English comes into its own, and Pakistan takes shape in the global imagination due to a clutch of trailblazing authors, precious little is being done within the country to encourage or promote, or for that matter, discover new talent.

With this in mind, the first Life's Too Short Short Story Prize was announced in March 2009, made possible with the help of the Zohra & ZZ Ahmed Foundation, and advertised nationally. With no entry fee, and offering Rs 100,000 for the winning story along with an opportunity for publication, the prize was judged by a panel comprising Mohammed Hanif, Daniyal Mueenuddin and Kamila Shamsie.

Submissions started in a nervous trickle, two a day, three a day, leading to a nerve wracking few weeks. Deadline day was an avalanche. We had eight hundred entries to read and whittle down for the shortlist.

International interest in Pakistani writing has come as a mixed blessing. More people are inspired to write, but sadly a fair amount of them are inspired to write utter guff—to cart around the self-conscious burden of representing the mythical Real Pakistan. The best works were small, close and intimate, crafting believable, fleshed-out characters, narrating stories with conviction and skill, stories close to the writer's heart, stories that made their point with subtlety and precision. The judges and we, the Life's Too Short team, are delighted at the standard of entries that made the final selection, published here for the first time, with Sadaf Halai coming in first for Lucky People, with first runner up Aziz A. Sheikh for The Six-Fingered Man and second runner up, Rayika Choudri for Settling Affairs.

Alongside new fiction and original photography, the Life's Too Short Review includes an exclusive extract from the forthcoming Rabbit Rap, Pakistan's first graphic novel, by Musharraf Ali Farooqi & Michelle Farooqi. We also feature an excerpt from the serialised story Challawa, translated from Urdu by Mohammed Hanif, making this the first time an English translation of this genre of popular "pulp" fiction has been published locally.

While it is tempting to look to writing from Pakistan for insights into a troubled country, we hope that this collection is read simply as good writing, conflict zone notwithstanding.

Faiza S. Khan and Aysha Raja, Karachi, 2010

New Fiction Baby

Mehreen Ajaz

He asks the clerk at the counter for a pack of Camel Lights, hoping to distract him from the lubricant and the pregnancy test in front of him. He doesn't really need the lubricant, or the Lights, just the pregnancy test, but he figures the lubricant says, "We're totally in control of this possible pregnancy," and the cigarettes say, well, cigarettes are just cool.

She hasn't really missed a period yet. It's a couple of days off is all. They don't want to take any chances though. He's pulled out enough times for there to be chances. He's only twenty and she's barely nineteen; both new to sex, both clumsy and awkward. She is small but big-boned, lonely and full of secrets. She watches romantic comedies that make her heart hurt with longing and desperation. She pines for movie-screen romance, for long and passionate kisses and even longer and more passionate nights of lovemaking. She wants to be like in the movies, tall and thin and beautiful and witty. She wants love so desperately, but can't imagine why anyone would choose her, man-hands and small brain and love-handles and all. When he kisses her for the first time, she thinks it's a joke, because he is the most beautiful boy she's ever seen. He kisses her and the butterflies in her stomach and the lightness in her head almost make her pass out but the whole time she's thinking he's fucking with me oh god oh god why is he fucking with me?

He's tall and intelligent and oddly self-centred. He's socially conscious but does nothing about it. He talks of being an anarchist, and his house is strewn with anarchist theory but it's just theory, and all he does is watch TV all day and eat all night. He goes out with one of her friends before he kisses her. Her friend claims they did nothing but go to a movie where he tried to hold her hand, and then he drove her home, where he tried to kiss her goodbye. She doesn't like him, her friend says, for either of them. He's not her type. He's self-destructive, can't you see, her friend says. When she expresses interest in him, her friend tells her, you're being stupid, the dumbest thing you could do for yourself is go out with him. She accuses her friend of harbouring secret feelings for him, of not wanting her to be happy. They are no longer friends.

It happens by chance, the time they finally do go out, after the friend-date debacle. She meets him through a friend who brought him over one night when she was at home. He is depressed and she's lonely and wants desperately to fall in love. He stays long after the friend leaves because he sees that she finds him attractive and he wants to milk it. He takes her home at one in the morning and lets her pick the movie. They watch *Pretty Woman*.

He tells her to go to a gynaecologist, "It's only normal, you know?" He wants her to get a birth control prescription. Months later, and she's still not been. She's embarrassed of her hair but she doesn't want to shave. He won't use a condom, he says it feels better without. It's hard to get pregnant, he says, look at all the people that are trying. Pregnancy has a pretty easy solution. She agrees. She ignores it and pretends he's in love with her.

They do things together. They have a lot of sex. Boring, short, selfish sex, but she doesn't know the difference really, and besides, she's madly in love with him. Then he leaves her for college with, "I'm really sorry, but I don't really like you like that, you know? I mean you're nice and all and I love hanging out with you but I need something else in my life right now. You know?"

The night he's scheduled to say goodbye to her he's late. Held up by his friends. That night she gets drunk for the first time, takes fourteen shots of cheap raspberry vodka and vomits all over the bathroom. When he finally comes to see her, only minutes before he has to leave for the airport, she's passed out fully-clothed on her roommate's bed. He wakes her and she mistakes him for her neighbour.

Two months later he's back. He drops out of school because his drinking habits keep him awake at night and asleep all through class. He finds her lost in freshman year, holed up in her dorm with no friends and twenty extra pounds to hate. He finds her, the only person that loves him like this, and they get drunk and have sex.

And now they're back here again, she's back to pretending like it could work again, and he's buying her a pregnancy test and just trying to keep himself together.

He brings the CVS bag out to her, his mind thinking furiously of ways to get out of this. She's sitting in the car, waiting. As she reaches into the bag she has a thought. "Do we really want to know whether there's a baby growing inside me?"

She doesn't mind if there is. She's been thinking about this while he's been gone. She wants his baby. After all this, she thinks, maybe he'll finally come around to actually loving her. He can't not love her. She's seen the movies. The daddy always comes around. She's already started thinking about the baby. What the baby will do for her life. How the baby will smile at her with love. She hopes her baby has his skin, his eyelashes, his good looks, his intellect. She hopes her baby has her teeth and her hair. She hopes her baby isn't going to be an alcoholic, like her baby's father. She hopes her baby loves her. She hopes her baby will make her baby's father love her.

"I mean, really, do we?" It's a test.

"Yeah, I really think we do."

"I don't, really."

She'd rather forget about it all until it actually comes. If it comes.

"What happens if I am pregnant?"

"Well you're not keeping it." He looks over at her. "You're not, right?"

"No."

She wants his baby, but he doesn't want her baby.

"We'll get an abortion."

She's reading a book called *The Abortion*, by Richard Brautigan. She hasn't really made up her mind on whether or not she likes it. The baby's father in the book is a librarian at a funny kind of library. People write their own books and give them to this library. She doesn't much like the narrator. He seems too incredulous and sheltered for her liking. He impregnates a beautiful woman and they fly to Tijuana for an abortion. The whole thing costs two hundred dollars. This is where she stopped. She wonders how everything turned out.

"Abortions are kind of expensive. I was going to buy an iPod with my next paycheck."

"Don't you have health insurance?"

She doesn't.

"Even if I did I'm not letting it pay for an abortion. My parents would disown me in a second if they found out. Besides, I doubt insurance would pay for an abortion anyways."

They try to stop thinking about it. It's just an abortion. It'll work out. Everything works out for them, they're lucky.

"Drink water, so you'll need to pee."

He turns up the music and she melts into the seat of the car surrounded by the bass and his voice rapping his anxieties away.

She asks him to take her to the museums. Museums are romantic places to be, intimate, and with nothing but beauty on either side. There's an Andy Warhol exhibit, she's heard. She likes Andy Warhol, although she's not much of an art critic. She likes things that are bright and colourful and modern and she loves anything beautiful. She likes neon Post-it notes and flowers. She puts flowers in her hair to make herself look pretty. When she sees something beautiful she wants to hold it, to have it, to touch it. She wants to put everything beautiful onto her body. The flowers don't suit her hair. She loves beauty so much she has a tendency to spoil it.

As he reverses into a parallel parking space round the corner from the museum she sees a flowerbed growing a few feet away. She gets out of the car before he pulls on the brake and breaks one off; she plugs it behind her ear, gives her hair a shake and turns to him shyly. Coyly, she waits for him to see her. He asks her which way they're headed. As they wait for the walk sign to flash, he looks down at her and sees her frowning. He notices the splash of colour. He pulls her toward him and kisses her hair, because he knows this is what she wants.

Her heart flutters.

"Do you want a pretzel?" she asks.

"Not really." He is silent and sullen for the next few blocks. They come to another vendor and she stops. She buys a pretzel, an ice-cream sandwich, and a hot dog.

"Sure you don't want anything? I'm starving."

He mumbles something about them already having eaten.

"Okay, let's go."

Once she's finished eating they walk into the museum. They are frisked. Her bag is checked and she's frightened, for an instant, of what the security guard might see. She looks up at her baby and she sees that same flash in his eyes. But they left it in the car, that bag that holds their future.

They view everything quickly. He is brooding and a bore; she can't seem to lift his spirits. She tries slipping her hand in his and stroking it suggestively but he takes his hand back. Forty minutes later, they are on their way to his house, windows down and music blaring when he drives into a car with broken brake lights at thirty miles an hour and their heads jerk back and bounce off the headrests and the front of his car crunches inward as their seatbelts dig into their shoulders and into their stomachs and in that second she thinks he's gonna die and he thinks Jesus Christ I'm gonna die and she thinks oh god no not my baby not my baby and he thinks I don't want to die and they stop jerking and they sit in silence and they collect themselves.

"Jesus Christ, what the fuck?" He curses to hide the terror. "Goddamn motherfucker."

His hands are stuck fast to the steering wheel. He wants to get out of the car desperately but he can't seem to stop playing the accident over in his mind. Each time he sees the crunch he freaks out again. He looks over at her and his desperation to get out doubles. "Oh fuck me."

"Oh my god," She can't look at him. Her heart is about to burst from beating in fear. My baby, she thinks. My fucking baby my baby my baby please not my fucking baby. She clutches the narrow box, her heart beating hard, her heart pounding against her ribs. She thinks my baby might be dead could my baby be dead is it alive enough to be dead?

He gets out of the car, finally, frantically, to yell at the motherfucker who can't keep his brake lights in check. She is panicking while he's exchanging insurance information and angry words. She is waiting for him to return so they can drive away so they can go back to his place so they can leave these wrecks behind so she can pee into a cup and look for even the faintest blue cross that would give her any kind of hope that he'd stay with her, that maybe he'd do the right thing. She is thinking irrationally. She is thinking my baby will make my baby stay. My baby will love me. They both will. She is desperate for this baby now. She needs it.

"Are you okay?"

She nods, mute.

"God, what a fucking asshole. He's so gonna pay for this. Douchebag. My neck's killing me. I hate him so much."

He tries to lose himself in this new direction of hate and anger and tension. He tries to focus on the car and on driving and on getting home safely. He has almost forgotten. But she hasn't forgotten. He drives home cautiously, jerkily, like every car he sees is an accident waiting to happen. Her right hand is sweating, clutching the test so tightly. Her left hand is damp and cold.

When they reach his apartment she jumps out of the car before he can park it. She waits anxiously by his side as he struggles to stick the key in the lock. He is badly shaken up, but does not want to show it. In the bathroom, finally, she opens the box slowly, pulls out the slim plastic tube and stares at it, her bladder only half-full. She wills herself to urinate. Ten minutes, now. She lays the test on the sink. Ten minutes. He knocks on the door.

"Hey are you okay?"

"Uh-huh… I'm gonna be in here a while."

Nine minutes. She thinks of the day they met, how she put nail polish on him because they were bored and how he took her home and how they watched *Pretty Woman* and then kissed all night. She thinks of the first time he took her shirt off, the first time she took his shirt off, the first time they took everything off, and how scary that was. She remembers how he guided her through it, like, it's ok, we don't have to do this if you don't want to, we can wait more if you want to but she said no; she said she wanted to do it more than anything, and she did. She thinks of how painful it was, that first time. He was her first, she thinks. She remembers begging him to keep the light off but he said no, and she said I'm fat and you'll think I'm ugly and he told her she was beautiful, that she wasn't fat at all. She realises now that he hasn't told her that in a while, and she resolves to lose some weight after the baby. She thinks of everything romantic he's ever done for her, like when he holds the door or when he bought her gerbera daisies because she had no money and she had her heart set on having them. Seven minutes. She thinks of how lonely she was before she found him, of how he made her life into the kind of romance she's always dreamed of. Six minutes. She thinks of the first time they tried on the word 'baby' for size. Hey baby. In her mouth it sounded like cardboard. Baby. C'mere baby. Baby, could you hand me another beer? It sounded foreign in her mouth, much too advanced a term of endearment for her. She went from nothing to baby, to serious-couple, I love you baby, I love you too baby. No sweetheart or honey to ease the transition. She wanted to be like them, those people on TV, they say it so easily. It comes smoothly, like they've been saying it since they could talk. Baby.

But the saliva in her mouth softened it. To damp cardboard. Baby baby baby baby baby. To sopping wet cardboard. Baby. To mushy cardboard paste that moulds around her tongue.

He did it too, then. He'd been watching the same TV shows. She'd say hey baby and he'd say hey baby right back. And it sounded perfect, like they'd been born saying it. He called her baby and the word wrapped her in a cocoon of safety until, "I can't do this anymore." And her mind exploded. And her heart weighed down her body. And he said, "Baby, I'm sorry."

She thinks how much she loves him. She thinks of the e.e. cummings poem, it goes "I carry your heart (I carry it in my heart)" and she thinks, that's me, that's me and my baby, me and both my babies. I carry your hearts in mine. Four minutes. She thinks she's glad her baby is bringing them together again. She thinks about what she would do without him and it pains her to realise that she couldn't live without him. She looks at the plastic tube sitting in the little plastic cup with so many minutes before it tells her fortune. She unlocks the door.

Outside the door, he's sitting on the bed waiting for her. She comes out silently, crying. He does not know what this means. He gets up and he holds her. He thinks this is what she wants. She sobs into his shirt. He pulls her onto the bed, still holding her. He waits to hear anything. He waits to hear what he wants to hear.

"It's positive."

He says nothing. It's like he hasn't heard. She says it again.

"Positive."

"Positive." He's looking at her incredulously. She whispers it now.

"Positive."

He's touching her face. "Positive?"

"Mmhmm."

His hands are working the buttons of her work shirt. She can't seem to stop crying. He's managed to unhook her bra. She's grasping around for tissues. He's taking off her pants when she runs out of tears. She can't seem to find any reason for why he's doing this. He wipes her remaining tears with his fingers and starts to kiss her. She doesn't know how to respond. She pulls away and looks away. He says, "What, what's wrong?"

She wasn't expecting this. A positive test doesn't end like this right away. She knows she's naïve in her expectations of him but she's not this naïve. She knew to expect some coaxing, some threats, some anger. Unasked-for affection comes rarely from him; it hasn't come at all recently. She doesn't know what to do. She starts to give in. She thinks, why question what she's always wanted. She thinks, I knew it would work. She thinks how much she loves her baby. She thinks of all her baby has done for her already.

He pulls her from the bed. He makes her stand in front of him and he looks at her. He looks her up and down and thinks how much he doesn't love her. He thinks that no matter how much he tries, he couldn't bring himself to. He thinks about where he'll go next to get away from her. He takes her hands and smiles at her. She smiles back happily. He holds her by the arms. One last time, he calls her baby.

New Fiction
Settling Affairs

Rayika Choudri

A week later, they could still smell her in the flat. The conspicuous smell of a living person: of lavender soap mingled with sweat and urine and Eau de Cologne No. 4711. It was strongest in her bedroom, where the sun slipped slowly down the wall—from ducks in a park lake on to an aluminium walker—lingering in between to disrupt the careful symmetry of her bed. Medicines had already been sorted through, some lying in the bin, others removed to be utilised, distributed. All that remained on the night table were squares and moons in the dust.

Zaheer sat on the edge of his chaarpai in the room behind the kitchen, waiting for the kettle to boil. He would be able to hear it easily over the pedestal fan, just as he could hear the occasional scrape of the sofa and chair in the lounge, where they sat and spoke in low voices.

It had become harder to breathe in the flat. A fortnight had passed since he'd cleaned any of the netting on the windows and it was growing opaque with grime. Begum Sahib would have become shrill: I will not tolerate it, we are not pigs. Things got dirty in Rahimyar Khan too—utensils grew layers of grease, bedding turned stale—but he had never taken it personally. So when he first came to work with Khalida Begum Sahib, he had balked. Subjected to her shaking finger, wrung out by her methods, he used to complain to his wife on the phone. How much time moneyed people had to spend on unimportant things. Which end of the bed sheet went at the head and which one at the feet. One sponge for dishes, one for glasses.

The kettle rang out just then with a trill of steam.

In the lounge, Hameed and Yasmin each shifted position slightly when they heard it, as though it was a signal for action, but all they could bring themselves to do was to cross the other leg or pull a little closer to the table. Hameed picked up a box of playing cards, lifted the cover and emptied them into his palm. They were waxy and turned slightly outwards, with a red criss-cross design on the picture side. He peeled a small, black-and-white photograph off the bottom of the box. "I never asked her why she kept it here."

Yasmin knew the photo well enough to bring its image to mind without looking: their father, standing against the railing that ran along the bank of the Salzach river in Salzburg. The small smile with which he looked into the camera—that of a serious person, one who seldom got carried away. "I suppose she always thought of Daddy when she used them."

"They did play a lot. Bridge and rummy. Mummy loved her rummy."

"And her solitaire."

Distant traffic was a constant sound in the flat. Louder however, were the pigeons that cooed and shuffled along the window sills.

"She refused to come live with me. I asked her so many times." Yasmin leaned forward. Her hand hovered for a moment over the table, as if she had forgotten what she wanted to do with it. Then she began to tug at the crochet mat to straighten and smooth its creases.

"I asked too."

"I know. It was just the way she was."

"Maybe we didn't make her feel welcome."

"I don't think that's true. And anyway, I don't think there's any point in talking about this."

Zaheer brought the tea tray in. He placed it on the table, obstructing Yasmin and Hameed's view of each other.

"Thank you, Zaheer. Can you just check if Saif wants anything? And take these for him." Yasmin piled a few biscuits with red centres onto a saucer for her grandson.

"How about a game in Mummy's name?" Hameed shuffled the cards.

"Hameed, I think we'd better discuss what we're going to do with her things."

Zaheer looked from one to the other as he finished placing the tea cups and saucers in front of them. There were elements of Khalida Begum Sahib in each. The high foreheads, the bump in the bridge of the nose. But they were both larger and blunter.

He was about to exit when he heard Yasmin say, "And with him? What should we do about him?" He paused. They had forgotten he could understand them, that she had taught him some English. He continued out the door, but then pressed himself against the wall outside.

"Can you give him a job?" Yasmin asked.

"Doing what? We've already got all the servants we need."

"Hameed, he's been working with Mummy for so long. Eight years, nine years? I can't even remember."

Ten, Zaheer thought, staring down at the plate in his hand and then staring past it, so the red jam dots doubled and blurred into stars.

"Take him with you then, if you're so worried about it."

"Don't be absurd. I can't take him with me to Abu Dhabi."

"But you assume he'll want to move to Islamabad? Ali lives here," he pointed out, referring to Yasmin's son.

The stars became jam again and Zaheer pushed himself off from the wall. He went into the dining room, where Saif sat working on his third grade mathematics. "Anything more, Baba?" he asked, putting the plate down before him.

"Can I have some cheese and toast, Zaheer?" the boy asked him eagerly.

Zaheer smiled. He had obviously rummaged through the fridge and had seen the bowl of cheese. He'd made it the day before and, when Yasmin saw the yogurt in muslin cloth hanging from the cabinet handles, she asked him about it. He had said he was making it for a cousin, who also lived and worked in Karachi. The yogurt was his own purchase, the cloth was Begum Sahib's. He hoped Yasmin Bibi didn't mind. She didn't and accepted his explanation, even though it wasn't entirely true.

He had bought the yogurt with some of the money Khalida Begum Sahib had given him for that month's groceries. And it wasn't for his cousin. He made it because the process always pleased him. Water straining out of the yogurt, drop by drop. Collecting in the bowl below until, hours later, it presented itself as the only thing standing between one form and another.

The doorbell twittered and he went to see who it was.

"Munawar Sahib," he announced to Yasmin and Hameed, as the landlord of the flat squeezed past him into the lounge. Hameed rose to his feet while greetings were exchanged, and he instructed Zaheer to bring another cup of tea. The stocky landlord, however, waved his hand. "That's all right. I'm not here long, just have to sort out some matters."

"If it's pending rent, don't worry. We'll take care of it," Hameed said, sitting back down.

"Yes, I'm sorry to have to bring it up, but I thought you might both be leaving Karachi soon," the landlord said, still standing. "Also, I wanted to know when the flat will be empty."

"Empty?" Hameed frowned. "The lease is ours now, isn't it?"

Munawar shook his head. "No, it terminates under these circumstances."

Yasmin caught Zaheer's eye. He had been waiting at the doorway in case of further instructions and she gestured that he could go.

"Well that's ridiculous!" Hameed exclaimed behind Zaheer. "My daughter's moving in here in a few months."

The dining room had a small balcony connected to it, and while Zaheer knelt before the net door with a rag and a mug of water, he could hear Munawar and Hameed speaking loudly. Once or twice an incredulous laugh, a placatory hum from Yasmin. He wondered whether he should start looking for another job immediately or whether to wait until after he had gone home to visit his family. He missed his wife and his three boys. He had not seen them for over a year—a longer stretch than usual—but this time he hadn't been able to leave Khalida Begum Sahib. There had been no question of a temporary replacement.

On the balcony, the budgerigars chirped in their cage and Zaheer leaned out to see if he had left enough seed for them. There were two pairs, all hues of blue and green and yellow, with black marks like splattered ink. He had always known her to have budgerigars. A little life and colour, she'd say. He watched as a blue budgerigar wriggled out the hole of one of the earthenware birdhouses and flew to the perch opposite.

"Saif Baba," he called out, from where he squatted in the doorway. Saif turned in his seat and Zaheer gestured for him to join him.

"What?" Saif asked as he stepped past Zaheer and knelt in front of the cage.

"Look inside their house," Zaheer pointed. "Can you see?"

Just then Munawar strode past the dining room. "I'll be in touch," he called out forcefully over his shoulder and the door slammed shut behind him. It could have been the wind.

Zaheer turned back to see Saif's frowning face light up. "I see them! The eggs!" Sure enough, in the hay-strewn base of the birdhouse, six eggs shone, smooth and white like ocean pebbles.

"They all need a new home," Zaheer said, gently detaching the seed bowl from the cage. He glanced sideways at the boy and added, "someone to take care of them." Saif pressed his nose to the bars of the cage, trying to get a better view.

Khalida Begum Sahib had lived till the age of eighty-three. She was all habit: marmalade and toast for breakfast, rest after lunch, meals on a tray in the lounge unless she had company. She was content with her outdated VCR and favourite films on videocassettes that grew lines across the picture from wear. She made Zaheer watch them with her, insisting they would help his English: "Dr Zhivago", "To Kill a Mockingbird." But it was "The Sound of Music" that she had loved the most, given it had been filmed to a great extent in Salzburg. The funny nun and all those children running, dancing and singing through hillsides, around fountains; they made her eyes shine with memory. Those gardens were a twenty-minute cycle ride from our home, she'd say. And Zaheer, seated on the ground or on his stool, would look from her to the screen, trying but never quite able to digest this incredible idea.

He wouldn't have guessed from looking at her, but her father was English, a businessman who met her mother in India, married and converted to Islam. She was twelve when they moved from Bangalore to London. At twenty-one, she married an Indian and they lived for some time in London. Until, that is, his work in the shipping industry took them to Austria—an Austria that was slowly getting back onto its feet after the war. In Salzburg, she said, you can be swimming in a lake and gazing at snow-capped mountains all at the same time.

Fifteen years later, she moved yet again—this time back to the region, to Pakistan. Not before I took this photo, she told him, as he shuffled cards for their game of rummy. Then she peered over her glasses at him: you must miss your wife and children.

Before each annual holiday he took, she'd buy presents for him to take back for them. Cloth or bags for his wife, toys and books for his boys. It was an excuse for an excursion in her old Charade, of which he was also the driver. He went into shops and markets with her, not to help her choose, but because her knees shook over steps and because, in a crowd, she looked as delicate as a leaf, as though any moment she might be swept away.

Late at night, the sound of heavy breathing from the spare bedroom gave Zaheer license to drift around barefoot in the flat. All the rooms were dark and the ticking of the lounge wall clock followed him everywhere.

She had deteriorated so suddenly over the last year.

Zaheer had always known her to be on medication for her bones, but she began to complain of more aches and weakness, swapped her cane for a walker and became slower in every way. And, as though it was connected, she started to forget things more often. So much so, that she needed to keep notes so she could take her medicines properly. So much so, that she forgot even to write them and needed Zaheer to keep track of her daily pills. She called him to help her get out of bed every morning when all her bones were at their stiffest. She started eating meals in her bedroom. She lost weight. She stopped spending the occasional afternoon at Ali's house and settled for seeing him, his wife and Saif once a week when they came to her.

Once, a long time ago, Zaheer had dared ask her why she didn't live with one of her children, and she had looked at him so coldly, he wished he could pull his words back into him like a rope. She'd never been a burden to anyone, she said, and she wasn't going to start now. As long as she could help it, as long as her means would allow, she would live on her own terms.

So he didn't say anything, even though all the changes alarmed him. And he could see they alarmed her too. There was a look that had crept into her face that said she was trying to swim against the current, against where it was taking her.

Zaheer pushed open her bathroom door and switched on the light. A dank smell rose from the pipes and a bucket lay under the lower shower taps. Small, flower-shaped mats had been plugged into the floor to make it less slippery and a sponge and two smaller mugs hung from the side of the bucket.

Three times a week, a cleaning lady came to do the heavy sweeping and mopping and, for the last few months, Khalida Begum Sahib had paid her extra to help her bathe because she could no longer do it on her own. But the weather was hot and sticky and three baths a week would not do, so Ali's wife helped with the fourth. But it was still not enough. She called Zaheer to her bedside and gripped his shoulder: you are like my son.

He stood outside the bathroom, while she sat on her stool and soaped the front of her body and then called for him. She would be bent over with her back towards him, her arms crossed in front, and he would come in and drip soap water from a mug all over her back—the part she couldn't reach herself, since she could barely raise her arms. With another mug of plain water, he washed it all off, not touching her, but thinking that if he did, if he could wrap his hands around her emaciated body, she would gather up into feathery skin and cartilage.

Then he would drape the towel over her back, turn away while she wrapped herself in it, and help her back to the dry ground of her bedroom.

I don't need a nurse, she shouted on the phone to her children. So Yasmin had said she was going to come earlier than usual—both she and Hameed used to visit once or twice a year, with or without their spouses. And when she arrived, she took over the bathing from Zaheer, although perhaps she didn't realise it.

One morning, Zaheer heard Yasmin cry out from her mother's bedroom and he went running to find her kneeling by the bed. Then he saw Khalida Begum Sahib lying on the ground, eyes shut, mouth slightly open. Call an ambulance, Yasmin had shouted. But by the time it arrived, she had already bled into her brain and died.

Zaheer switched the bathroom light off. Street lamps cast a dim, yellow glow in the bedroom window and, somewhere outside, a car roared away into silence.

Rocky hills, clumps of bush and patches of crop drew up and fell away again from the bus as it trundled down the highway. And occasionally, fragments of wooden skeleton—what used to be a shed or a shack—sailed past Zaheer's window, lingering in his thoughts.

In the end, the flat was conceded to Munawar and, bit by bit, things were sliced up and divided. Clothes, furniture, appliances and trinkets were either dispatched into various family households or sold or given away. Hameed kept all the paintings. Saif asked for the birds. Yasmin spread out all the photographs on the bed, loose or in albums, so they could sort through them. And Zaheer stepped in and out of it all, cleaning, packing, loading into vans and trunks of cars. In and out of their arguments as well, which took place mostly through gritted teeth because neither wanted to seem grasping.

On his last day at the flat, Yasmin had given him three months' pay and the promise of good recommendations. Ali will ask around for another job for you, she told him. He thanked her and said that when he returned from Rahimyar Khan, he would go to see Ali Sahib.

Zaheer drew some papers from his pocket and sifted through them till he found what he wanted: a photograph of Khalida Begum Sahib. He had pulled it from an album when no one was in the room. It was a few years old and of her alone, sitting in her corner of the sofa with a plate of cake in her lap. She looked unready for the camera, unsmiling. He didn't think it would be missed.

"Who's the amma?" the man next to Zaheer peered over at it. He was burly and lodged thickly between him and the aisle.

"My Begum Sahib," he replied, putting it back in his pocket.

The man stared at him for a moment. Then he shrugged and leaned back, closing his eyes. Somewhere in the bus, someone cleared their throat as though about to spit, while Zaheer rested his head against the window. He looked out at a quiver in the highway, where the horizon lost all definition in the beating sun.

New Fiction
Mir Sahib's Hairdo

Danish Islam

Early one morning, Mir Sahib looked at his image in the bathroom mirror. He observed every feature with curiosity and admiration in turn. He saw the trademark mole on his cheek and his freckle-free face: a cherished family trait. Best of all, he still had a bushy moustache and a full head of hair, having lost not a single strand, he suspected, in his sixty years. But age hadn't spared him entirely. Each hair on his head was white. What had once been a forest of jet was now snowed under. And it wouldn't bother him either, without the constant nagging of Begum Mir.

"Baba ji, put on some Kala Kola" was Begum Mir's pet phrase these days. Today, Mir Sahib decided he could no longer take it. He snuck his wife's bottle of Kala Kola into the bathroom with him. He opened the bottle and looked at it, thinking in the Shakespearean style, "to be or not to be." He realised it had to be. He started to neatly cover his hair with the paste, till there was a knock at the door. It was none other than Begum Mir.

"Mir Sahib," she called, "are you planning to stay in there all day? Hurry, you have to go to the NADRA office to get your ID card made. Don't you remember?" she asked through the door. With her voice grating on his nerves, Mir Sahib sped up the process, quickly spreading the Kala Kola over his hair and moustache. Rushing through it, he was unable to keep a steady hand, which proved to be a disaster. His hair ranged from the darkest black to a duller black with intervals of white. He was a conundrum of colour.

When Mir Sahib finally exited the bathroom the first person he saw was his wife. Begum Mir saw black and at first she gasped with joy, he had finally listened to her, but her gasp soon turned to laughter when she looked closer. She laughed and laughed so loudly that the entire household gathered to see what was so amusing. While they were more subdued by necessity than Mir Sahib's wife, everyone, he felt, was guffawing on the inside. The children, who wouldn't dare laugh outright at an elder, reddened with glee. His brother and sister-in-law did a better job of hiding their amusement but there was a distinct expression on their faces that said, "What in God's name have you done, Mir Sahib?"

Breakfast was a quiet affair. While the reaction of his family had been demoralising, his walk through the street would prove a greater humiliation. Mir Sahib was a well known figure in the neighbourhood and recognised by everyone on the block. As he walked he saw life slowing down as he passed through the street, eventually coming to a halt. Men on balconies stopped reading and peered from behind their newspapers, women stopped mid-chore. All eyes were on Mir Sahib and they all seemed to say, "What in God's name were you thinking?" To add insult to injury, a dog stopped to look at him. It was the same look, "What in God's name were you thinking,

Mir Sahib?"

Soon Mir Sahib made it to the busy main road and walked a few hundred paces to the closest bus stop. On the way, he realised he'd forgotten to bring his spectacles with him. This would make it annoying for him to recognise his bus by its number. There was only one person at the stop, a girl, probably waiting for her bus to college, he thought. Mir Sahib sat in the men's section and looked towards the oncoming traffic. It was a bit blurry so he peered intently. After five minutes, the girl stood up and stomped furiously towards him.

"You should be ashamed of yourself! I am your daughter's age!" she spat out. Mir Sahib was at first confused and speechless. Apparently while he'd been looking at the traffic the girl had thought she was being looked at inappropriately. "You have been staring at me ever since you got here! Just because you have coloured your hair does not mean that you have become any younger, or as a matter of fact, any more charming!" she said, storming off. Never in his wildest dreams had Mir Sahib thought that his hair would cause him such grief. All he could do was grind his teeth in anger.

Soon enough, his bus rolled along and he boarded as slowly and carefully as his knees allowed. It was quite packed but the bulk of the standing passengers were disgorged at the next stop. Now only Mir Sahib was left standing. This seemed odd to him as usually a younger passenger would offer him his seat. Today, for some reason, he noticed none of the passengers even looked at him, let alone offering up their places. A man of Mir Sahib's age came aboard. His hair was overwhelmingly white. A young boy stood up and Mir Sahib moved forward at seeing a seat vacated. But then the young man motioned towards the old man behind Mir Sahib, leaving him standing there. This was a great blow to Mir Sahib. He had been overlooked before just because of the colour of his hair. This is racism in a complex way, Mir Sahib thought. He stood for the rest of the journey.

Mir Sahib disembarked at the NADRA office. Usually people have to stand in line outside the office to queue for their identity cards but Mir Sahib was not among those poor souls. As it happened, Rehan, a former student of his had been appointed head supervisor at this very branch of NADRA. Mir Sahib approached the security guard.

"Tell your head supervisor Rehan, that Mir Taj-ud-Din is here to see him." he told the guard, slipping him 20 rupees. The guard returned shortly to escort Mir Sahib to the supervisor.

Rehan looked at his former teacher in what could only be described as awe. "Yes Mir Sahib, what can I do for you?" he asked, politely. "I'm here to apply for the renewal of my ID card, but you know my arthritis makes it so difficult for me to stand in those wretched lines. Please take my token and sort it out for me, son," said Mir Sahib, handing the token over. Rehan summoned his peon and sent him off with the token, telling him to bring tea and biscuits too.

Rehan tried to suppress his curiosity. But after a minute or so of discussing the weather and the queues, he had to ask, "Sir, why the new look?" "Child, do you remember in school I used to call the boys who tried smoking, speeding and other forms of hooliganism out of peer pressure idiots? Well today I have become one of those idiots myself. My wife is the real culprit, I did this to stop her nagging," said Mir Sahib tersely.

Rehan thought idly of his fellow students whom he'd be regaling with this story later in the week. "Sir," he said, as humbly as he could manage, "I can get you through the queues but there is the small matter of your photograph…" Mir Sahib had forgotten. He didn't even bother to object, just clucked and prepared himself to be captured in black and white—and that was just his hair—for posterity's sake. Following the ordeal, he returned to Rehan's office. "Well you can't walk around this city looking like that. I fear your reputation is not the only thing that you may lose. Let me help you, sir." Rehan bent down and fumbled for something in the drawers of his desk. He came up with a baseball cap with NADRA written on front. There was only one problem with this solution. Mir Sahib had never worn a baseball cap before and it was a matter of pride for him. He did not care for American clothing, nor any western clothing. Only a turban or a Jinnah cap had ever conquered the head of Mir Sahib. But since desperate times call for desperate measures, personal standards had to be abandoned.

After a little chit-chat, a cup of tea and lots of biscuits, Mir Sahib left NADRA with his new identity card. Soon, he was back on a bus and again there were no vacant seats but the cup of tea had sufficiently fortified him for his journey. He disembarked at his usual stop but did not head home. Instead, he took the path to his barber's shop. The barber had known Mir Sahib all his life and when he saw his newfound jet blackness he knew Mir Sahib's visit was a cry for help. The barber removed the baseball cap and assessed the full scale of damage.

"Mir Sahib, what have you done!? If you had wanted your hair dyed you should have come to me first. What am I supposed to do about it now?" asked the barber. "Can't you level the colour tone or mellow it down?" Mir Sahib pleaded. "Well, adding more blackness may further ruin things. I can try to mellow things down but the procedure may be a bit drastic," said the barber. "How drastic?" asked Mir Sahib. "Well, I can bleach your hair and get it back to that majestic white." said the barber. "Will it work? Will I have my hair back the way it was?" asked Mir Sahib, hopefully. "No guarantees Mir Sahib. But we must just do our best," said the barber. Mir Sahib couldn't help but feel that he was taking some pleasure in his discomfort.

The barber left Mir Sahib on the chair and went across the road to his house, returning with a bottle of bleach. He applied the bleaching agent to his client's head and started rubbing it over his moustache using a cotton ball, telling Mir Sahib to keep his eyes tightly closed. Finally after half an hour the barber stopped. Mir Sahib opened his eyes. The first sign that things had not gone well came from the look on the barber's face. It was a loud and clear "oops." It was with some trepidation that Mir Sahib looked into the mirror. He narrowly avoided a full-fledged sob. As promised, his hair was no longer black. But it wasn't white either. Mir Sahib was now blond.

This was a catastrophe, but this was not all. His moustache was of a different colour to his hair. He then noticed the second blunder. Some of the bleach had trickled down his forehead onto his eyebrows, whitewashing them along the way. Now instead of eyebrows, Mir Sahib had a zebra crossing above his eyes.

"Shave every hair," hissed Mir Sahib.

Without awaiting further instructions the barber got his electric shaver and began motoring through Mir Sahib's blonde locks. He cleared the head, he cleared the eyebrows and then as he was halfway through the moustache the power went off. Mir Sahib was not amused. He sat and waited for the scheduled hour of power loss to end but it was not to be. The power didn't return and when the evening was underway, Mir Sahib had no choice but to leave, shred of moustache still intact.

It was now pitch black outside and Mir Sahib was thankful for being able to reach his home without further ridicule. It was with some relief at seeing the end of this sorry episode that he knocked on his front door. One of Mir Sahib's grandsons came to the door, but seeing an unknown bald man through the peephole he went running to his mother without opening the door, as instructed upon seeing strangers. "There is a bald man at the door," said the child excitedly. His mother went to the door, and saw in the dimly-lit street a strange bald man with a quarter of a moustache. She approached Begum Mir, the head of the household, who warily approached the peephole.

"Who is it?" she asked. "It is I. Open the door, woman," replied Mir Sahib. Begum Mir looked through the peephole but did not open the door. She went to her son Riaz.

"Son, there is a man at the door. He sounds like your father but I think it is one of those beggars who shave their heads to pose as cancer patients," said Begum Mir. Riaz went to the door. "Who is it?" he said, sternly. "It's your damn father and if you don't open this door right now I will break it down myself and shove my walking stick up your bum," shouted Mir Sahib, officially at the end of his tether. Riaz quickly opened the door to let his father in. Mir Sahib's face was red with anger. This was not an uncommon occurrence but usually the redness was restricted to his face. This time his whole head was also glowing with heat. Riaz didn't know whether to worry or giggle.

"What a joke!" stormed Mir Sahib, "A man comes to his own house and is asked a hundred times who he is. The children I can forgive but Begum Sahiba, are we still strangers after 35 years of marriage? If I recall correctly this was pretty much what I looked like two years ago when we came back from Hajj. Now what are you looking at me for, give me some food you fools, I am hungry. It is a good thing I have my students to feed me or else I would have surely starved after all the work I have done today. Half of the work was convincing you idiots that I am your father..." went on Mir Sahib all night till it was time for bed.

It took two months for Mir Sahib to grow back his snow forest. During this whole time no one dared to ask why or how his hair had been shaved, or for that matter, his eyebrows. Most importantly, Begum Mir never nagged Mir Sahib ever again.

Excerpts
Challawa

Sabiha Bano

Even though I own an air-conditioned car, I often take the bus. Why? Not everyone would be able to understand. Certainly not because it helps my digestion, nor because I am partial in the least to the lewd remarks passed by drivers and conductors. It is a matter of the heart, a tender emotion that can only be felt, not explained. It definitely cannot be felt by men. Only women can sense it and very few women at that. The famous Greek poet Sappho, for example, would have appreciated it.

The weather was romantic that day. Tiny grey clouds were scattered along the sky like *dhunki hui* cotton wool. A cool breeze blew stealthily like someone approaching their lover's home unannounced. In this kind of weather my heart becomes restless, and I start to hum the couplets of Faraz and Nasir. I set out in search of a lover and if I don't find one then I have to reluctantly settle for a drink by myself. Once I start drinking, I have to keep going till my body and soul drown in that bottle. It was my good fortune that not only was the weather clement that day but all was well in the city—by which I mean that girls' colleges were not closed. I must remind you that I speak of the days when the mother of the nation had been defeated by General Ayub in a rigged election and, after widespread protest, schools and colleges had been shut down. Fortunately for me, they had recently reopened.

I set off in my own car, parked it on Elphy and strolled over to the Regal bus stop. As I walked, I could feel hundreds of warm, penetrating eyes on my body. Propositions were whispered, someone whistled, but I ignored it with the contempt it deserved. I boarded a bus which I knew would be making stops at various girls' colleges. It was packed, like all the city's buses, but the ladies' section in the front had only two occupants. One was a middle-aged Memon woman possessively holding on to her bags. The second was wearing the kind of burqa which had once prompted a Makrani donkey cart driver to say, "Oye, parachute! Move out of my way!" At the next stop the ladies' section welcomed two fresh arrivals—a mother and daughter. The mother was in a veil but the daughter—about twelve or thirteen—was still too young for purdah. I looked at her small breasts and could feel the tang of guavas on my tongue, a taste I hate. I prefer oranges, fresh, round oranges. The bus stopped at a girls' college and a rabble of butterflies poured in, clutching their books to their chests. There were fair ones and dark ones, short ones and tall ones, veiled and open faced, experienced and green. You should have seen my wandering gaze! It was a sumptuous spread, but I found it difficult to settle upon one. After all, no one has ever faulted my taste.

My next hope was a girls' school five stops away. The bus conductor approached me and as I bought another ticket I started to worry about how

I would arrange for a girl I liked to take the seat next to mine. Lady Luck was on my side. By the time the bus reached the girls' school, the neighbouring seat had been vacated. I opened up my legs a bit to claim it. At the stop, an avalanche of young ones barged in. I looked over at the newcomers with anticipation. A few of them reminded me of overripe melons. Now, when a fourteen-year-old girl reminds you of overripe fruit you know society has failed in its basic civic duties. Puberty before its time has its causes in specific societal evils, but if I start lecturing you on the flaws of our society, I'll never get round to my own story.

I looked around impatiently. As I zoomed in on a fifteen-year-old whose breasts met my preference of size and shape, my heart blossomed. I felt a fluttering in my chest and my person experienced a form of light intoxication. I reached for her hand, grabbed it and pulled. "Come, baby, come sit here." I moved my legs together to make room for her. She thanked me and sat down. Her voice didn't have the kind of music I was expecting. But while her voice was ordinary, her body wasn't ordinary at all. Her complexion was the colour of a white flower smudged with saffron. She wore the standard girls' uniform, blue frock and white shalwar. I casually put my hand on her thigh and asked, "Where do you live, baby?" "Nasirabad," she responded, shyly. I liked her shyness. Bold and extroverted girls are usually more delicious in bed but it's difficult to get them there. The shy ones are easy to seduce.

Because the bus was so packed with people, no one noticed my hand on her thigh. "What's your name?" I asked. She told me her full name, which included her father's name. Now, her father is a respectable man—and has already suffered so much that I don't wish to add to his miseries by naming him—so let's just call her Farrukh. "What class are you in?" I asked, increasing the pressure on her thigh. "Matric," she said. I slowly started moving my hand. Shivers ran through my body. I glanced at Farrukh, her face had started to grow flushed. Now she put her left hand in her lap to try to deter my hand but when I persisted her resistance broke down. I can only assume she was experiencing the same tremors in her body that I felt in mine. When the conductor arrived, I paid for Farrukh's ticket despite her protests. "Don't be so formal, doll," I said and she blushed at that. As her face reddened, I felt an irrepressible desire to take her into my arms. As my hand strayed even further, her breath quickened and her eyes glazed over. "I'm also going to Nasirabad," I whispered. "I had to meet a friend there at five but my car broke down in Saddar and you know how difficult it is to find a cab at this time. Men can run around and look for cabs but what should us women do? I had to take this bus." "Which car do you have?" Farrukh's meekness was tinged with genuine curiosity. "A Mercedes," I said casually, adding, "if you like, we can go for a ride in Clifton in the evening. Perhaps I can show you some of the paintings I make at home?" Farrukh smiled and looked uncertain. This would be easy.

As the Mercedes rose into the driveway, Farrukh cast an admiring glance over the elaborate exterior of my mansion. "Leave your books in the car," I said. I took her by the hand and started to climb the stairs. She had no idea how impatient my longing was. As she stepped onto the plush carpet, Farrukh cried out. "You are so rich!" "Not that rich," I smiled. "But whatever's mine is yours." I showed her around the house and she seemed very taken with the crystal chandeliers and works of arts. At length we arrived at my studio. Before I entered, I instructed my special servant to make sure nobody disturbed us. The studio had everything I needed. Farrukh was very impressed with my work. She praised my paintings to the skies but all I could think about was how much I wanted her in my arms.

"Would you like some orange squash?" I asked.

"Sure."

She had begun to relax. I made two glasses of orange squash, put a dash of brandy in hers, and poured a whole shot in mine.

"Baji, you make such nice paintings," she said.

"Not Baji, call me Bano. I told you what my name was so you'd use it."

"Wow. So I should call you by name?" She seemed mortified.

"Yes, we are friends. Right?"

"That doesn't matter—after all, you are older than me," she said, innocently sipping her drink.

"You can still call me Bano."

Farrukh finished her drink without noticing the bitterness of the alcohol. I fixed her another orange squash, this time with more brandy. Farrukh took the glass and finished in a few small gulps. She rubbed her throat and pulled a face. "What is the matter, honey?" I put my hand on her shoulder. "The squash was a bit bitter."

"Oh, how can squash be bitter? Want another?"

"You are so funny," she said, giggling. She was a bit tipsy, her eyes had reddened.

I put the glasses away, took her hand and said, "Let me show you my bedroom."

My bedroom is adjacent to the studio. Farrukh was over the moon when she saw the décor. She touched everything with the gentleness a child employs when playing with bubbles. When she reached the bed, however, she pressed down hard on the mattress. "Oh god, it's so soft." "Sit down," I said tenderly. She collapsed on the bed and sank into the soft mattress.

Her face was red and she looked like she had been tickled. I sat down too. "I feel a bit tired," I said, leaning on her. "Why don't you take a nap?" she suggested.

I put my arms around her and pulled her down with me onto the bed. Farrukh squirmed. I pressed her into my chest, kissed her glowing cheek and whispered, "I really, really like you, Farrukh." "I also really, really like you, B-B-Bano." Her breathing quickened. I could feel her blossoming youth on my soft breasts. When my right hand slid under her jumper, Farrukh squirmed again. "What are you doing, Bano…" she asked in a husky voice.

"I am loving you, my darling. You love me also. Don't you like me?"

When my hand reached the small of her back, she let out a small cry. She closed her drunken eyes and let her body lose all resistance. This was my experience at work. Every time I do this, girls give up all resistance. I put my thirsty mouth on hers. Her lips were like petals, tender and juicy, and I sucked them softly of their nectar. Occasionally I bit gently with my teeth and whenever I did, Farrukh let out a gasp.

My left hand passed over her neck and arm and reached her young, hard breast. With my right hand, I lifted her left leg and placed it on my hip. She was still wearing her pumps, which I removed and threw to the side. I slowly began to press her toes, then her soles and slender ankles. Then my hand crossed all barriers. Though Farrukh was a bit dazed by the brandy, my touch drove her wild. She had closed her eyes with shame but her body was on fire. It was making demands even she didn't understand. Every pore of her body cried out. *I am burning, quench my thirst. I am on fire, cool me down.* When I was certain of no resistance, I started caressing her leg through her shalwar. I reached her knees and then higher, higher… Farrukh lay still as I struggled with the knot in the drawstring of her shalwar. The redness of her face told me that her desire had reached its peak. I shivered as I saw her youthful abandon. I quickly released myself of all my clothes and clung to her as if I wanted to melt into her. Now her hands had started to make shy little moves. I guided them to my breasts and pressed down on them.

I wanted her to be as uninhibited as I was but this was her first time and I had to guide her hands to pleasure myself. Fresh youth collided with a ripe body. As our intoxication increased we felt as if the stars were breaking out of their galaxies and falling down around us. Both bodies were drenched with sweat but there was a fragrance to this perspiration. Moment by moment, our bodies were reaching their peaceful destination. Farrukh was no longer a stranger to her desires. She had acquired knowledge and she knew she was getting exactly what she had wanted. There was no part of her that my lips had not touched. Our madness was increasing as, clinging to each other, we rolled around on the spacious bed, trembling, twisting, shrinking, expanding. Contented sighs filled the silence of the room. Thousands of mysteries of our life were being revealed. The rosebud at last announced its bloom.

Our breath had scattered and every pore was exhausted. Our entangled bodies lay still and lifeless. We were at peace. Neither of us wanted to move. After ten minutes I broke the peaceful silence.

"Farrukh."

"Hmm," she said, her eyes remaining closed.

"Ok, get up now."

But Farrukh didn't rise or open her eyes. I removed my arm from under her neck, got out of bed and put on my gown. Then I walked to the cupboard and took out another gown. Throwing the gown at Farrukh, I said, "Wear this. Your uniform is all rumpled. It'll have to be ironed."

Translated from the Urdu by Mohammed Hanif

New Fiction
Lucky People

Sadaf Halai

Asma Iqbal, wringing a dishtowel around her hands, stood in her kitchen and stared out of the window, past the thin patch of grass they called the lawn, at the laundry hanging in Mrs. Hassan's yard. But she noticed neither the laundry that Mrs. Hassan's maid had left out overnight nor the plastic toys scattered on the ground like confetti after a party. In her mind's eye, Asma was watching her husband Tariq sitting in his office, at a desk burgeoning with dusty blue files and capless ballpoint pens, carefully drawing a line with a steel ruler in his accounts register.

Asma sat down at the counter that separated the TV room from the kitchen, unfurled the newspaper, releasing it from its rubber band, and turned to the Classifieds section to look for the advertisement they had placed.

RESIDENTIAL RENTAL PORTION

Gulshan-e-Iqbal, block 17, ground floor, near National Stadium, 500 square yards, living room, 2 bedrooms, kitchen, bathroom, line water, parking.

When Tariq first suggested that they rent out the ground floor, Asma had resisted the idea. She had a hard time explaining to him that she was fiercely proud of the fact that they lived in a house with both an upstairs and a downstairs, and a small garden in the front with a flowerbed full of periwinkles. It wasn't a flat, and it wasn't a small house, and this to her felt like an achievement of sorts. Nine years ago, when she saw the house for the first time as a young bride, Asma had imagined slowly filling its rooms with carpets and teak furniture. But the travel agency where Tariq had worked for ten years had floundered, not flourished, and the house did not look anything like the pictures that Asma would carefully snip out of issues of magazines bought at the Tuesday bazaar.

She looked around her. The sofa set was as old as the house, and in the seat the blue corduroy had faded to a lighter colour. Once white and feathery, the lace curtains were now yellow around the edges. And despite her best efforts, she'd been unable to completely erase the scribbles that Omar, her seven-year-old son, had made on the walls. Their resolute crayon shadows—one-dimensional houses with windows like sad, vacant eyes— had lingered on.

Asma listlessly flipped through the rest of the newspaper. It was always bad news: hotel bombings, power outages, drone strikes in South Waziristan. She rarely read the newspaper, which bothered Tariq immensely. You need to know what's happening in the world. He'd chide her in the same tone he would use to tell Omar to get off the computer and read a book instead. Even though Asma was bothered by the terrible things she saw on the news, she'd inherited her father's lack of faith in Pakistan. "When I came here from

Uttar Pradesh as a child," he often told her, looking away into the distance as if he was watching that train snake its way out of India, "I thought I was going to some place wonderful. A place like heaven. Not this," he'd say with disgust.

Asma glanced up at the wall clock in the TV room. The words Speedy Travels stretched out from the 9 to the 3, in tall letters, partly obscured by the moving needles. She had an hour to shower, change and drive to Omar's school in P.E.C.H.S. before two o'clock. He had maths tuition in Clifton at three-thirty. Instead of driving all the way back to Gulshan-e-Iqbal, they usually had Happy Meals on Tariq Road. She'd sit in their car—a white Suzuki Alto—outside the tutor's 1,000-square-yard bungalow and wait for Omar to get done with his maths class.

Before leaving the house, Asma stopped at the bottom of the stairs. In anticipation of the new tenants, Tariq had hired a carpenter to build a makeshift plywood door to cordon off the staircase from the downstairs section. The workmanship was shoddy, and where Asma ran her hand over the door's surface, sharp burrs of unfinished wood grazed her skin. She paused to look at herself in the oval mirror that hung next to the main door. Under her loose lawn kameez, the bump was tiny. It was impossible to tell she was three months pregnant.

Later that evening, just before Maghrib, Asma was in the kitchen making hunter beef sandwiches when Tariq called and said, somewhat breathlessly, that a couple was going to drop by around eight to see the house. At first, Asma said nothing. She was holding a knife in her hand and the smears of mayonnaise on its blade were starting to drip to the floor.

"Yes, that's fine. What time are you coming home?"

"Jaan, I'm really sorry but I have to finish this paperwork today, I don't think I'll make it home by then. Do you mind showing them the place yourself?" he asked.

"But you said February was going to be a slow month and the month is almost over. You've been coming home late every day."

She heard him sigh. It was what he did when he was too tired to argue with her.

"Okay. Sure, I'll do it," and she hung up.

An hour later, when the doorbell rang, Asma smoothed her hair back into a ponytail and told Omar to come downstairs with her.

"No, Amma I want to watch TV" he wailed in that voice that always set her teeth on edge.

"All right but you'd better finish your homework before you sleep!" she shouted back at him.

She'd expected the couple to be older, middle-aged, with a child or two in tow. But they looked like college students, barely in their twenties, well-dressed, smiling and good-looking. They introduced themselves as Nadia and Khalid Murad, and their easy confidence made Asma uncomfortable. The girl was dressed in blue jeans and a short kurti, and the boy was wearing khaki trousers and a white linen shirt. A large ring on the girl's finger caught the light from the bulb above the door. Her hair was curly and wild, and large sunglasses perched on top of her head kept it from falling into her eyes.

Asma walked them through the downstairs section. It was clean but bare, and she wished there was more in it, a painting on the wall, or a potted plant in the corner perhaps. The living room was empty, except for a few cane sofas with beige cushions.

"I like those," Khalid said, pointing toward the French windows that looked out on the garden.

"Yes, they're lovely," Nadia agreed, but her tone was uncertain. She wore high heels that clicked on the chip-marble floor.

The kitchen was ordinary and the countertop was cracked in a few places.

"What do you think baby?" Khalid addressed the question to Nadia. He stood with his hands on his hips, as if he were surveying a vast territory. Even though his clothes looked expensive, he wore scuffed sneakers; he had a tousled and carefree look about him.

"Can we renovate the kitchen?" Nadia asked Asma.

She blinked. She hadn't expected them to like it, let alone consider moving in and making changes.

"Yes, I don't see why not. I can discuss it with my husband tonight."

Once they'd checked the bedrooms and the bathroom, satisfied with the plumbing and the fixtures, they thanked Asma for seeing them at such short notice and promised to call the next day. They explained that they'd been living with Khalid's parents but really wanted a place of their own. This arrangement would fit their budget and they'd be twelve minutes away from Shahrah-e-Faisal, where Khalid worked in a bank.

"Our friends think we're crazy for moving all the way out here," Nadia said, while she opened her purse to pull out a silver case full of visiting cards. Asma noticed a red and white cigarette box nestled in between a hairbrush and a notebook.

"Here you go," she said with a flourish. "My useless husband has left his wallet at home," and they both laughed. Asma joined in, even though she was not amused, and secretly baffled that such a young girl had a visiting card and carried her own pack of cigarettes.

"I love your earrings by the way," Nadia exclaimed, pointing to Asma's ears.

"So traditional." She said the word traditional as if it were a special state or a rarefied thing.

After they left, Asma made two chapattis for Omar's dinner and kept the rest of the dough aside. She packed his lunchbox with the hunter beef sandwiches for school the next day and checked his Islamiyat homework for spelling mistakes. Then she waited for Tariq to come home so they could eat the chicken saalan she'd cooked that morning. She watched the TV on mute, the Prime Minister's mouth moving without sound, like a fish inside an aquarium. And she looked at Nadia's card for a long time, turning it over and over in her hands.

Nadia Murad

Art Director

Aperture Magazine

The Murads did not move in quietly. Over the course of a week, a Suzuki pickup made countless stops at the house, dropping off furniture, a fridge, and brown cartons sealed with masking tape, the words "This Side Up" and "Handle With Care" scribbled on them with a black marker. Tariq joked that the young couple owned enough things between the two of them to solve the refugee crisis. Asma said nothing. From her bedroom window, which overlooked the garden and the entrance to the house, she watched the Suzuki unload lamps that looked imported and Persian carpets in colours like indigo and maroon.

Nadia shouted shrill instructions in Urdu to the men who had been hired to transport their possessions. Asma complained to Tariq about the noise, but when he suggested she close their bedroom window, she murmured something about fresh air and insisted on leaving it open.

A week later, Nadia dropped by, unexpected, with a spinach quiche on a blue platter. Asma thanked her for the pie.

"It's a spinach quiche, from The Pastry Palace," Nadia corrected her.

The older woman nodded without understanding. She'd seen the bakery on Zamzama but had never eaten a quiche before.

Asma led Nadia into the drawing room; it was rarely used and smelled stuffy. The walls were lilac, and though it had seemed like a good idea when they had the house painted several years ago, Asma no longer liked the colour. Nadia sat down on the sofa stiffly and placed her handbag by her feet. It was embellished with alphabets. Asma often admired such bags on the arms of mothers who picked up their children from Omar's school.

"How has the move been?" Asma asked.

"Oh, it's been quite an annoyance. I had to take a few days off from work and we're short-staffed as it is…"

"At the magazine?"

"Yes!" She smiled and settled back into the sofa. "I'm the creative director." Asma detected the note of pride in her voice. "It's a young company, I'm practically the oldest person there."

"The oldest! How old are you?"

"I'm twenty-nine."

"Twenty-nine! Well, from where I'm sitting you look very young," Asma said.

"No, no, I agree with you," Nadia said, holding up her hands in a gesture of defeat. "But for the kind of work I do you have to be young otherwise you become extinct. But if I were a housewife and wanted children then age wouldn't be such a…" Her voice trailed off.

"Don't you want children?"

"I don't think so," Nadia replied, shaking her head. "Khalid and I have talked about it. I think he wants them." She raised her eyebrows in exasperation. "But frankly that just isn't for me. I mean, there's so much I want to do. I don't think I have the time."

Asma didn't know what to say. It had never occurred to her that having children was a choice, or something you might not have the time for.

After getting married, she'd never used birth control, and when Omar was born two years later, she'd accepted his birth as the next stage of her life. Now, almost seven years after having Omar she was pregnant again. It had taken her so long to conceive a second time that she'd resigned herself to having just one child. Her mother would tell her on the phone that at least she'd borne Tariq a son; it would soften the blow of not having any more children. But Asma had been secretly relieved that she wouldn't have to endure, once again, the morning sickness and the sleepless nights that had accompanied her first pregnancy. However, as soon as she grew accustomed to the thought of having time to decorate the house or visit her parents more often, a lab report from the hospital confirmed that she was pregnant.

"I see," she said flatly, and left it at that.

"I have to travel a lot for my work," Nadia explained. "I'm a photographer and that requires me to be mobile, you see. Last year I was in Italy and there are no elevators there." She rolled her eyes. "I couldn't possibly have gone to half the places I did if I had a child with me! Have you been? It's like heaven."

"No, I haven't." Asma had visited India in 1994 with three friends from university. They'd taken the train and stayed with relatives in Bombay and watched Hindi movies at the Regal Cinema. It was her first and last trip outside Pakistan.

"But your husband is a travel agent!"

"Yes he is."

Neither woman spoke for several seconds. When Asma broke the silence by offering to make some tea, Nadia politely declined and said she had some work to do.

"It's really nice to have you as neighbours," she told Asma at the door.

"You're welcome," Asma replied. "And thank you for the pie."

"The quiche," said Nadia, smiling, and disappeared into the darkness of the stairwell.

Later that night, after Omar and Tariq had gone to sleep, Asma tried the quiche. She chewed it slowly, trying to identify its ingredients.

And then she ran to the bathroom and vomited into one of the blue polythene bags she kept inside the sink cabinet.

Toward the end of Asma's fourth month, the Murads turned their attention to the garden. They hired a part-time gardener to mow the grass. Orchids in coconut shell planters, strung up from the neem tree, swayed lazily in the wind. To Asma, the flowers looked extraterrestrial; she felt suspicious of their violent colours and their petals that looked like mouths. One evening, she watched Khalid from her bedroom window stake small garden lights into the lawn, along the edges of the flowerbed. After Maghrib, the lights, like Japanese lanterns, began to glow. When she asked Tariq what they were, he laughed and said they were solar lights. "The thing of the future," he said.

In early April, the Murads had a garden party on a Saturday night. A catering company was hired to barbecue chicken tikkas and Behari kebabs on an outdoor grill. A divan strewn with red cylindrical pillows was placed under the neem tree and mosquito coils in red terracotta platters were scattered around the garden. The solar lanterns sparkled. Asma looked out at the garden from her bedroom window and her heart sank. In all the years she'd lived in that house, the view from her bedroom window had never looked like this. She'd assumed the Murads would be too wrapped up in their jobs to bother with the garden. But they'd accomplished in a matter of weeks what she hadn't been able to in years.

The guests started to arrive at around ten. The sound of high-pitched voices began to waft into her bedroom. Omar was asleep: Asma had forced him to go to bed early. Tariq was sitting on his side of the bed, wearing a white mulmul shalwar kameez, reading last month's Reader's Digest. His glasses were perched on the tip of his nose. Asma was at her dressing table, wiping away traces of kajal from under her eyes with tissue paper and cold cream. She watched Tariq in the mirror. The light from the bedside table illuminated half his face. She knew he would sit there for another half hour, calmly turning the pages, and then he'd remove his glasses, turn to her and say "Shabba khair" and promptly fall asleep, his soft snores filling the air between them.

The voices from the garden grew louder. Asma placed the dressing table stool next to the window and sat down. There were about ten people in the yard, and they looked like they were Nadia and Khalid's age. All of them held cigarettes and wine glasses or green beer bottles. The women wore tight jeans with tops that revealed their arms and necks. Nadia, incandescent in a bright yellow blouse, flitted from guest to guest, and Khalid stood behind a table littered with bottles, pouring out drinks. He seemed to be enjoying his job immensely.

"What are you doing?"

Asma turned to face Tariq. He'd put the Reader's Digest on the side table and was watching her quizzically.

"Nothing."

His expression softened a little.

"Do you want to join them?" he asked.

"Are you crazy? This is a drinking party! Besides, we're not invited. Anyway, I don't understand why these people moved to Gulshan in the first place..."

"Of course we're not invited," Tariq replied matter-of-factly, as he reached over to turn off the bedside lamp.

Asma turned back to the window. Someone had put on some music and a few couples were dancing. Every few minutes, they would switch partners. Asma felt foolish for watching them, but she couldn't look away. She sat there for about an hour. As the evening wore on, the crowd grew drunker and louder. Soon the lawn was littered with paper plates and bottles full of cigarette butts. A few girls were sprawled out on the divan, laughing uncontrollably. Some people had left. Nadia looked tired; she'd removed her high heels and was sitting by herself, in one corner, drinking from a glass bottle, her knees pulled up to her chest. Asma watched her for several minutes, and wondered what she was thinking.

The next morning, Asma woke up from a bad dream. She sat up in bed and picked up the phone from her bedside table. It rang several times before Nadia answered.

"Hello?" Her voice was heavy with sleep.

"Nadia, it's Asma from upstairs."

"Jee Asma." She sounded annoyed.

"Nadia, I know it's early but I just noticed the garden is a mess. My parents are visiting in about an hour. I'd appreciate it if you could have all the litter removed by then."

There was silence on the other end. A man's muffled voice said something in the background.

"I'll get it done." The phone clicked shut.

Tariq opened his eyes and squinted in the sunlight streaming in from the window.

"What time is it?" he mumbled.

"It's 8:30."

"You didn't tell me your parents were coming."

"They're not." She walked over to the closet and opened it. Most of her clothes were now tight for her; for weeks, she'd been meaning to go to Tariq Road to buy fabric for new shalwar kameezes.

"Then why would you tell them that? It's Sunday morning!"

"Have you seen this place?" she snapped, waving her arm in the direction of the garden, surprised at the anger in her voice. "It's filthy!"

Tariq stared at her, his eyes wide with exasperation. His face was puffy from sleep and his hair stood up in little tufts. It had been turning white for a few years. When they'd gotten married, the six-year age difference between them hadn't seemed like much. But now he was forty-two. Most of his hair had turned white, and his joints would hurt at the end of a long day.

She expected that he'd scold her, as he often did when he thought she was being unreasonable. But instead he shook his head, his face full of disappointment and left the room without a word.

The next morning, after Tariq and Omar left the house, Asma emptied the contents of her bedside table drawer on to the floor. She had a doctor's appointment in a few hours and was looking for her Patient ID card. Sifting through the receipts and hairclips and crushed blister packs, she found an envelope marked "Spare Key Downstairs". She told herself she could slip the envelope under the Murads' front door: that way, she could avoid meeting Nadia altogether. That morning, when she'd looked out of her bedroom window to see if Omar's school van had arrived, she'd seen the Murads' grey Honda Civic pulling out of the gate. Nadia was sitting in the back, wearing her over-sized dark glasses, and Khalid sat in the passenger seat, next to the driver, his cell phone pressed to his ear.

Standing outside the Murads' front door, Nadia took the key out of the envelope. It lay in her hand, shiny and silver. She stared at it for several long seconds before she slid it into the keyhole and pushed the door open, her heart thudding painfully in her chest. What are you doing, she thought, but when she locked the door behind her, she noticed her hands were steady.

The first thing that caught her eye in the living room was a print hanging on the wall. It was a picture of a woman, seen from the back, crawling through a vast field of stubby, brown grass, toward a house in the distance. Underneath the image, it said "Andrew Wyeth The Museum of Modern Art, New York." The picture unsettled her. The thought of the woman crawling her way through that expanse of grass, the bony back, the thin arm outstretched toward the house: it filled Asma with a strange unease.

Next to the print was tall fern, and in the centre of the living room were low, white couches strewn with papers and files. Books and cartons were stacked haphazardly against the wall. Empty cans, cigarette boxes and an ashtray overflowing with cigarette butts lay on the coffee table. She opened the fridge, and wasn't surprised to find it full of Chinese takeout in clear plastic boxes. Of course she doesn't cook, she thought.

The bedroom was a mess. Clothes and shoes were strewn on the floor and the bed was a tangle of sheets and pillows. At the far end of the room was a writing table, and on it lay a black folder as large as a newspaper. Asma opened it; the inside cover said NADIA MURAD PHOTOGRAPHY PORTFOLIO in slim capital letters. She'd seen such pictures in the travel brochures that Tariq brought home from work: canals with delicate bridges arching over them, young couples sitting on benches or drinking from water fountains, their hair gleaming in the sunlight. As a young bride, she would imagine visiting the destinations advertised in the brochures, cities like Istanbul and Cyprus and Kuala Lumpur; she would run her fingers over the photographs of beaches and ruins and impossibly tall skyscrapers. But Tariq, despite his good intentions, had still not been able to take her anywhere farther than Skardu.

Asma didn't know anything about photography. In all her years as a commerce student at Karachi University, she had steered clear of the arts; she knew there was no point in taking a drawing class, or studying the classic novels like her friend Raheen. She would just end up making a fool of herself. But she'd watch the Arts students lug in their easels and ceramic pots and cameras, and wished she was more like them, and less like herself. Looking at Nadia's photographs, Asma felt a wave of nausea rise up in her throat, and she shut the portfolio and left the room.

She did not stop to inspect anything on her way out. After locking the front door shut behind her, she slipped the key under the door. She took the stairs up, two at a time, and walked into her bedroom. The things she'd emptied from her bedside table lay on the floor in a little heap. She found her hospital ID card.

Asma looked at herself in her dressing table mirror. Her face looked pale and there were dark half-moons under her eyes. She brushed the hair back from her face, and that was when she noticed that she was wearing one earring. She never took those earrings off. The gold hoops, embossed with red enamel—like her nose stud—had slowly become a part of her face. And now one of the earrings was missing. Her mind began to race. Had she dropped it downstairs? Was it lying on the floor in the Murads' bedroom? There was no way to find out; she'd already slipped the key under the door. If Nadia were to find the earring, she would recognize it.

Despite Asma's fear that Nadia would show up one day and shake the gold earring in her face, that day never came. Nadia did not drop in again and Asma, for her part, did not telephone or visit. If they ever ran into each other, in the stairwell or outside by the gate, they would nod and exchange a few polite pleasantries, but the conversation was always brief and stilted. On the rare occasion that Nadia and Khalid entertained, their guests stayed indoors and rarely strayed into the garden. She didn't blame them for not wanting to talk to her.

Toward the end of Asma's eighth month, Tariq came home from work one day, beaming, and told Omar and Asma that he'd gotten a promotion. They celebrated by going out for dinner that weekend to a barbeque restaurant in Clifton. Tariq booked a table on the rooftop of the five-storey restaurant; while they ate their chapli kebabs they gazed at the city that sprawled out beneath them, its tracts of darkness divided by light.

The final weeks leading up to Asma's delivery were spent turning the study into a nursery for the baby. After Omar was born, they had let him sleep in their bed for two years, and Asma was determined to not repeat that mistake. Tariq grumbled for a few days when his books and college diplomas were removed from the study and stacked into cardboard boxes and scattered with mothballs. But when Asma's mother dropped off a crib and some pink dresses with matching socks, he declared that the study had been a waste of space. "Who needs a study when you can have a nursery!" he announced, smiling magnanimously, with the air of a man who's discovered one of life's great truths.

Asma rarely thought about the Murads. She had stopped worrying if Nadia knew that she'd let herself into their home and she stopped feeling foolish for having woken them up on that Sunday morning, many months ago. And so, when Tariq told her one evening over dinner that Khalid had called to say that they were moving out in a month, she felt inexplicably sad. She'd imagined that such news would make her happy: it meant the return of her house and the garden the Murads had lovingly tended. But to know that they were going to leave with such ease made her unhappy for reasons she could not understand.

On the day of Asma's caesarean, Omar was allowed to take the day off from school. It was the last week of August. Tariq filled the Alto's trunk with cartons of mango juice, packets of digestive biscuits and an overnight suitcase in which Asma had packed her clothes and toiletries. Omar helped Tariq load the car and when they were done, he held his mother's hand and helped her down the stairs. The three of them looked at the house one last time, as if they were going away on vacation. Tariq slowly drove out of the gate, past the neem tree and the swaying pots full of orchids. They drove in silence. Omar was sitting in the back, bobbing his head to music he was listening to through earphones.

"Are you alright, jaan? You've been very quiet today." Tariq looked in her direction, one hand on the steering wheel.

"I'm alright," she said. "I was just thinking about the downstairs."

"What about it?"

"I'd like to renovate it after the Murads move out."

"Acha. I suppose it's all right. But the rent has really helped these last few months. It's been a convenient arrangement, don't you think?"

"Yes, it's been convenient." She chose her words carefully. "But I want it back. There are so many things I want to do with it..."

"Okay jaan. If it will make you happy." He slowed the car down at the broken traffic signal. A policeman wearing white gloves was trying his best to steer the traffic in the right direction.

Asma looked out the window. In the car next to theirs was a couple, young and well dressed, thin and beautiful, their eyes hidden, as always, behind large, dark glasses. She wondered if, one day, stuck in traffic, she'd look out and see Nadia and Khalid in a car next to hers, and she wondered if they would roll down their window and say hello.

"It will," she said, looking at Tariq. "It will make me happy."

New Fiction
To Live

Bilal Tanweer

I was sweating inside my mother's car in that freak lane, saying to myself, "Come on, come on," while glancing in my rear view mirror searching for her female figure to hurry along in my direction. All I saw was a man of densely hirsute armpits uncomfortably seated on a chair too small for his awesome behind and poking a scratching stick in the back of his vest. Opposite him a little left-over fire nibbled at the heap of burned garbage, giving off a rancid smell I knew well from memory.

It had been three minutes now and nothing had emerged from the corner of the lane. I hated every second of it. I tightly clasped the ignition key. You had to be prepared when waiting for a girl you've never really met before. I was in an old, clunky Suzuki FX, a matchbox of a car—but I could've been off with it in less than three seconds, and on a bet, out of the lane in the next five, pedestrians and incoming traffic notwithstanding. The car, was impossible to accelerate. But I had mastered that art as well—if you simply floored the gas pedal, no matter your timing with the gears and all, it steadied out at around 58 km/h mark, often dwindling to 55. I knew how to jack it up to 77-type and keep it there.

All this was beyond my mother's maddest dream, of course, this car being her lifeline. She had put four years of savings into it. She treated it like her ringdove; I thought it my fighting dog. I wasn't allowed to touch it, except in extraordinary circumstances. She was sleeping when I pushed the car to the end of the lane before igniting it and getting away with it. I had been waiting a long time to see this girl, Sapna, I had worked hard on it. I called her before leaving the house; she said she was ready. Planning within my mother's sleep schedule, I gave myself an hour to get back.

It took me fifteen minutes to reach the spot where she was supposed to meet me. She had explained her location with the crookedness of someone who did not venture out of the house much. "It is the second lane on your right, from the roundabout," she had said. Wrong. It was the third. I was saved the frustration because she had mentioned, just as a by-the-way, "Oh and you will see a metal-shiner's pushcart. You will see pots and pans. He just stands at the corner of my lane. Hehe. That's how I remember it myself." That's how anyone remembers anything in this city, where most streets don't have names.

I turned into the lane with the pushcart which was neatly heaped with black pots, along with another, smaller dump of grey, polished metalware. A man squatted on the pushcart, scrubbing a little pan. Her house was the third one on the left, the tiny white construction that occupied the tight space between two houses. For some reason, the house was named Patang, i.e. Kite. I spotted it without trouble. I slowed down the car to look for any suggestion of her through the windows. I didn't see anything, except maybe a curtain moving in the top room. But that could have been anything. I was supposed to wait outside the old yellow house with the black gate. She would come, she'd said, when she sees my battered blue FX pass by her house. That was the farthest she had come in showing her interest in meeting me in our one month of phone conversations—and I was happy for it. Well, girls are like that. At least at first. She was a shy one and I was actually quite thrilled to meet her. Finally.

Frankly, no matter how many times you did it, it was always nerve wracking to meet a girl for the first time, especially if you've already had intimate conversations on the phone. She was convinced I was madly in love with her. I was seeking to cement that impression, among other, better things. She'd seen me, of course—and probably liked what she saw too. We went to the same place for our after-college private tuitions that I had quit after two classes because I'd much rather spend that money on something more useful.

I fancied her from the moment I walked into that drab tuition centre—a dark, dusty, windowless room, lit with fifteen tubelights and furnished with secondhand chairs and desks from which nails poked out, and worse yet, full of boys who spent their school time working their asses off and still came to tuitions for extra-practice. Girls were too few, and perhaps that was the real reason why I left that place. She was pretty though. Wore a half-sleeved yellow kameez, had short hair that fell around her face when she bent forward to read, and she smiled all the time. Her deep square necklines made quite an impression on me and I studied her intently for my two sessions there. The second day she wore a khaadi-brown and even shorter sleeves, and I scrutinised the back of her taut, fine neck for the whole hour and a half, and was left with no doubts I was going to try her. She was small and beautiful and perfectly packaged to be taken home and played with.

I found it a little difficult to find her number, but I managed after bribing the registration handlers of that tuition centre. I called her. "I know you, and like you too. I just want to talk. Make friends." Probably she was confused. Most boys don't approach girls like that. They wait around, do idiotic things like passing snide remarks or acting loud and brash. She was suspicious at first, understandably, but then I gave her time, let her make the choices (at least that's how I made it look to her), left my number and told her she could call me if she wanted to. She did, of course. And the rest, as they say, is history of one month ago. She had many questions for me, many sadnesses of her own to report. She lived with her mother and a dying father (cancer, something like that) and her brother, who paid for both of them, routinely threatened to turn them or himself out of the house. Anyway, after a point, I didn't care much about it. There wasn't much I could do. I was her only male contact and I broke her loneliness in a way that was new to her. In less than a month, she had fallen in love with me, she believed. And I with her. As I said, the latter was her own subjective judgment with which I did not interfere.

Well, that's what it's really all about if one thinks about it. Conversations. You want to be understood the way you see yourself. Boys think girls are looking for something that they can worship—and they go on adding weight to their six packs and nine biceps and so on and all they ever end up doing is stand posing in busy markets. Jerks.

I took my eyes off the rearview mirror—I'd had enough of the man in the lungi who seemed to have located the spot of his itch and was resolutely scraping it out—and was checking the fuel tank indicator when the door opened abruptly. I was in shock for a second when a figure wrapped in a shawl jumped inside. "Let's go, let's go!" For a second, I couldn't move. But the next moment I was assured by the invasion of a perfume. Ah, she was prepared for it. The car screeched a little and in less than five seconds, we were out of her freak lane and on the main road.

She sat diagonally on the passenger seat facing me. My first thought was, "Do I look all right? I hope I'm not sweating." Well, I was sweating. But so what, she loved me—and it was all right for a lover to sweat. She took off her shawl. I got a chance to look at her—and ah, that yawning neckline. She saw me looking at her and smiled. I smiled too.

My plan was to take her to an ice-cream parlour with an empty second floor at that time of afternoon. We could improvise something there. And besides, I had little money and that was all I could afford. But then, I was a little nervous myself, and didn't want to appear abrupt, so I waited on the suggestions. She didn't say anything and we drove quietly. Finally, after a while, I broke the silence, "So, where should we go?" I asked.

She didn't reply for a few seconds. I was about to navigate her to my preferred spot, when she said, "I don't know… I want to go somewhere far where we could talk." Ah, yes. Talk.

At that moment, we had reached Shahrah-e-Faisal, the jugular vein of the city, and I was still thinking of something funny to tell her to break up this tension. I put my FX in the fast lane and pumped the pedal to top up the speed. I could feel the exertions of the engine. She sat with her hands folded and I felt happy that she was wholly concentrated on looking at me. Suddenly she blurted, "Why not go to the sea?"

Well, not a bad place to be but I knew it would be impossible if I were to get back in an hour. After being kicked out of school, I had been my parents' prime cause of insomnia for the past two years. My communication with them had collapsed when I was expelled for bunking. Things had improved lately since I had enrolled in an accounting degree diploma and we even laughed a couple of times but there was no way I could explain this running away with my mother's car to them. I had already broken the excuse-bank of friendly accidents and flying donkeys trampling me. I found it difficult to imagine how much further I could shatter them and what that would look like—"Yes, that's what I was thinking as well," I said to her. "Okay, let's go. You have time, right?" I was shocking myself. This girl had unanticipated effects on me.

"Haha!" I heard her crackle. "Yes, yes. I can be out for another two hours. But not more, okay?"

I smiled but with a tightening in the chest. I had noticed the man intently staring at us from the car next to us. I didn't know what the hell was up with everyone in this city. Why must you face distrusting stares and smiles from everyone if you have a girl next to you in the car? But again, that depends upon your car, if you have a shiny, sexy four-wheel drive, you may well be screwing her in there and no one would dare take any notice—well, that's an exaggeration, but really. If you are in a little broken car, well, everyone will screw you as you cruise. I stared back at the man who was staring at Sapna from the bus window on my right.

When I was at school, we swiped ink from our van window at passersby. We especially targeted old men, and young couples we suspected doing wrong by meeting each other in private. You jerked off your ink pen when you were close enough—and pha! You stunned them if your ink-lasso caught them on their faces. They usually broke into curses. Young couples were the most fun to target because they showed most reaction and could do least harm in return because they were tied with each other and would never come after you. There are exceptions, of course. In that sense, I was afraid someone like me from my own past would leap out and do what I did, or something like it, like fling an egg at the windscreen.

I looked around and told Sapna, "Turn up the window and lock the door." She seemed surprised, "Why, what happened?" she paused for a reply.

"Well, because it's my car," I said, suddenly irritated.

"I'm feeling hot," she retorted and rolled it up by an inch.

I realised I probably sounded patronising the way I ordered her. That act of hers of running away with me on a sore afternoon and the risk she took could have resulted in limbs broken by her parents if they found out. I knew she did this because, as she said, "I want to do what I want to do—not what they want me to." I had offended her sense of freedom. That act of being with a man (she loved) in a strange place was what she wanted to do. And I was happy for her, for my own reasons, of course.

That little disagreement caused silence. I already felt a little annoyed watching everyone gawk at her—the beggars, newspaper boys, flower-sellers at traffic signals—and then the horrible traffic. I hated the rickshaws and motorcycles. And I had to get back home too.

At the Cantt Station stop, where the traffic was crawling because the buses clogged the turning and bus drivers took their pissing breaks, I spotted Comrade Sukhansaz descending from a bus, almost falling out, actually. It scared the life out of me. He knew my father and would report me, I had no doubt. There was nowhere I could have gone—I was parked between the behind of a shiny black Civic and the front of another sexy car I didn't give a fuck about, and we were all standing there honking our heads off at each other. Comrade Sukhansaz stood in an aggressive posture, his fists clenched, looking at the bus that had dropped him off.

"Damn," I said, craning my head out of the window to block at least some view of it, "I think he's seen me."

"Who has seen you?"

"That guy in the red cap. He's an old friend of my father. Oh damn me. Don't look, don't look."

"So?"

Well, there went my first impressions of being a brave, brave boy from a good family.

He had seen me, for sure, but I pretended I did not see him. We were moving inches. You fight for inches on this city's roads. From afar and up close, you train your eyes to scour them and the rest of yourself to devour them. Drive and survive.

Fortunately, Comrade stood at a point after which the traffic smoothed out, and I raced past him. He had seen me for sure because he had his hand up, not as in stopping me, but waving to me.

We must have gone a couple of hundred meters and we were just starting to ascend the bridge on the left as soon as you cross the Cantt signal, when the blast occurred. Almost instantaneously something flew and smacked solidly into the back windscreen. The strength of the explosion was so terrible that for a second it shook the bridge we were on, and the car, which was already whining from its ascent up the bridge, lost power. Sapna's hands trembled and she turned around to watch the unforgiving spectacle unfolding behind us. "Don't look," I told her, as I pulled the handbrake to keep the car from sliding down the bridge.

The next few moments were vague and my hand fumbled with the keys and instead of turning it in the ignition, it seemed to be trying to understand it. I turned the key hard and almost shoving it inside the ignition. I anticipated the bridge would blow up next. My hands felt too weak and I was seething with anger. Why me? Why us? Why now? Why here? "Duck!" I shouted at her. "Hunh?" her eyes were stunned and glued behind us. The car came to life finally, but after what felt a long time. I dropped the handbrake and pumped the gas pedal so brutally the car squealed as it raced up the bridge.

Cars sped towards me from the other end of the bridge, the wrong way. No one seemed to have any idea about the location of the blast and those idiots were just madly tearing towards the site itself. A Land Cruiser almost rammed into the car from the side. Bastard. One thing was clear: no one was going to stop. From there on drivers drove with their hands on their horns, cutting through the traffic lights, and the traffic—everyone wanted to rush out from that centre of fire and hell behind them. Or towards it. They didn't care. Everyone wanted to be out of there.

I don't know how and at what speed I drove, but I drove it probably faster than I ever did and it was not fast enough. Nothing felt safe or far enough. And when we emerged onto the sea, it was sudden, almost out of nowhere, as if I had been driving in insanity without registering anything at all.

The sea was deserted at that hour. It was on my right, but I was looking to my left, suspiciously, at the apartments that stood stolidly, their dirty-yellow paint dependably crumbling as always.

I parked the car, there was no one around. We kept sitting in there. I pulled down my window, and the breeze rushed in as if from another world, our hearts pounded like kicks in our chests, and the whole stretch of the sea seemed something new. It was not the desert it always seemed, not the last bit of earth, where I made out with other girls in the backseat of the car without being under the watch of anyone. We heard the sea breeze as if it was haggling for attention.

"Who was that man?" she asked. That was the first thing she had said.

"Comrade Sukhansaz."

"What? Sukhan what? Is that even a name?"

"Well, he made it. Sukhansaz is an Urdu word for poet. Comrade is what the reds call each other. Like, brother. This guy gave up his name for the cause, apparently. Spent nine years hiding, underground. He was one of those few who didn't relent, unlike my father and his friends—didn't start an NGO or something. He had been coming to our house a lot for the past few months; he needed money for the treatment of his arthritis. He wanted to get new knees." I paused. "I remember a few lines from one of his poems," I said

My lopped head will shout
My ripped tongue will roar

Kill me, O bandits,
My death will be my beginning

"Heh. You know, just before he recited this poem, he said to my father, 'Jaani, when I am gone, and you want to think of me, smoke a pack of Kingston, or read this poem. I want to be remembered by this one.'"

"You think he died there?" she asked, coldly.

I did not reply. I was still quite deaf with the sound of the blast, and my hands were still trembling. I was thinking if I should tell her what flew to hit onto the back windscreen.

"Shall we get out?" I asked her.

We got off and leaned against the hot bonnet to face the sea. We did not make eye contact. Our hearts still pulsated with fear and our eyes were fiercely set on the sea. I felt her come close to me, the length of her arm touched the back of mine. Absurdly, there was a pink moon over the sky, looking like a faint dabble in broad daylight. The migratory birds crisscrossed and flapped like a film reel in the air. We stood like that for a long time, breathing, and then, suddenly, she slid her cold hand into mine and held it tightly.

It wasn't until that moment that I realised I needed comforting.

For the first time, in all my years of running here, I felt the sea in a new way. It did not seem like the end of the city.

Before setting off for home again, I went to examine the rear windscreen and found it as I feared, splattered with bits of blood. I had clearly seen what it was that hit us. I wished I hadn't. I fought with my memory and tried to imagine it to be something else, but there was no time for that.

I cleaned the blood with a rag dipped in the car's radiator water. I found more splatters on the backlights, on the roof, the bumper. Sapna identified a couple on the door. I disposed of the bloodied cloth by flinging it on the road.

As always, we couldn't afford to have anyone find out.

New Fiction
The Wedding

Sarwat Yasmeen Azeem

"You're doing very well," Sadia said, smiling at Farhana. The little girl was reading the children's section of the newspaper aloud to her cousin who sat cross-legged on the floor, chin in hand, mouth hanging open. Sadia put her hand under her daughter's chin and firmly pushed the girl's mouth shut. The other children were playing in the street and Khadija lay on Safia Begum's takht with an old chiffon dupatta tied tightly round her head.

Sadia stirred the vegetables and found herself listening closely to a ridiculous story about a candle that wept tears of wax. Farhana's voice was high and clear, and she read well for her age. She was an ambitious little thing and already so responsible! The younger children, Ammara and Faraz, came to her with their problems instead of going to their mother. She settled their quarrels, took them to the bathroom, and gave them their meals. She was their surrogate mother, and she was barely ten years old.

Sadia felt a surge of affection for the child—affection tinged with jealousy that Farhana was not hers, but the daughter of that good-for-nothing who lay snoring on the takht. She reached out and smoothed the short hair that had been carelessly cut at home. "What are you going to do today?" she asked the child.

"Tomorrow is the wedding, you know. I've got to get the groom ready, and I've got to get my clothes ready and I have to decide what colour bangles I'm going to wear," she explained. "Sobia, have you made the list of songs?"

Sobia produced a scrap of paper and presented it to her mother. The songs were listed in a large, shaky, untidy hand and filled with spelling mistakes. Sadia looked at the writing and immediately wanted to slap her daughter. What a useless child! She spent hours working with her, but Sobia still couldn't read properly, let alone write. And today, listening to Farhana sweep through the two-page newspaper with hardly a mistake, Sadia wanted to slap both girls; one out of frustration, the other out of jealousy.

"I'm wearing the new pink dress Ammi stitched for me and Abbu is bringing new bangles for me tonight. They're going to be the same colour as my dress," Sobia prattled. "What are you wearing?"

Farhana simply hugged her skinny knees and giggled as if she had some delicious secret to hide.

"Ammi, can I wear the green dress I wore last Eid?" Farhana asked her mother that night.

Khadija lay on her back with her arm thrown across her eyes and ignored Farhana.

"Ammi! The wedding is tomorrow! See? I've got the groom all ready," Farhana held up her grotesque monstrosity of a doll and pushed it into Khadija's line of vision. The doll was large and plastic and ugly as sin, with most of its original, bright orange nylon hair ruthlessly hacked off. Farhana examined it morosely. She hadn't wanted to do that, but everyone said since her doll was so big, it would make a perfect boy. Besides, Khadija had promised her a new doll weeks ago. "You will get me a new doll, won't you?" she asked anxiously.

"Farhana, get out of here before I throw something at you," muttered Khadija.

"But, Ammi..."

Khadija twisted over and reached down the side of the bed. She rooted around in the dirty darkness, fished out a dusty, pink rubber slipper and whacked Farhana on the arm. The child yelped at the stinging blow. Khadija grabbed the doll and flung it over the cupboard. "Now there won't be a bloody wedding so stop harassing me about your blasted clothes!" She shoved Farhana towards the door. "Don't show me your miserable face again, you hear! Let me catch one sight of you and it'll be a shroud you end up wearing!"

The next morning Khadija climbed up on a chair and groped around for the doll on the top of the cupboard. She dusted it off and then dragged a large tin trunk out from beneath the bed. It was filled with the good things they never used, where she stored the children's good clothes. She picked through the bundles knotted in squares of cotton cloth and found the pretty green dress covered with gold embroidery. Shaking the dress out, she went in search of her daughter.

Farhana was in the kitchen, standing on a broken wooden stool, making tea. "Come here, child." Khadija eased onto the takht in the veranda. She was a mess, her hair—with new streaks of silver in it—was scraped back into a ratty plait. The bright blue chiffon dupatta was still wrapped round her forehead. Her eyes were ringed with large, dark circles, her skin was a sickly, spotty yellow. Farhana nervously stepped close and Khadija enveloped her in a big hug. "Come, let's get the mother of the groom ready for the wedding!"

The wedding was enormous fun. All the little girls came dressed in their best, clutching enormous silver purses in their hands. They dressed the bride in a red satin outfit that was too big for it and had to be held in place with several rubber bands. The groom was wrapped in a scrap of ivory silk.

The girls clapped their hands and sang wedding songs. Razia's father threw himself wholeheartedly into the game and appointed himself the qazi so that when it was time for the nikah, everyone sat solemnly as he bent towards the doll with the eyes that blinked. Three times he asked the doll if she accepted the groom, three times Razia bobbed her doll's head up and down. "That is good," said Razia's father. He then turned to Farhana's doll and asked the same question. The doll's ugly orange head wouldn't bob, so Farhana had to lift it up and down three times. Everyone then hugged and congratulated each other while Razia's mother handed out dried dates and lumps of sugar.

Razia's father had gone all out to celebrate the wedding of his daughter's toy, even getting the food cooked by a proper wedding caterer. The little girls squealed as the platters of biryani and qorma were brought in. The hot sheermal was snapped up in seconds, and a mad scramble broke out when the trifle appeared. In the melee of it all, everyone forgot about the bride and groom until someone asked, "Who is getting food for the bride?"

A dozen little hands, adorned with tinkling bangles, stilled over their plates. They looked at each other. Razia screamed.

A frantic hunt for the bridal couple ensued. Razia began to blub. At last they found the missing dolls squashed under the little pile of sausage-shaped cushions reserved for the VIPs—immediate family of the bride and groom. Razia's doll with the blinking eyes was unharmed, but the groom had lost a leg.

Farhana received her broken doll quietly and everyone gathered round. They looked scared and confused. Someone tried out a couple of tentative sniffles, but Razia wasn't about to let them spoil the mood of her party.

"Shut up!" Razia lashed out at the gaggle. "What are you lot crying for? This isn't even yours!" She snatched the doll and efficiently informed everyone, "My Abbu will fix him. Don't you worry about a thing, Farhana." She stomped out to find her father who was standing in the street, buying mangoes from a pushcart. She thrust the doll at him.

"Can you fix this?"

He couldn't. The leg socket was so badly twisted that the leg just wouldn't go in. Farhana leaned over the pushcart and smelled the mangoes. She really didn't care for the broken doll; she wanted to finish eating the wedding feast. "It's okay, Razia. My father will get me a new one. Let's go back."

When the girls had eaten as much as their little stomachs could hold, it was time for the rukhsati. The groom's party stood outside the door and the bride's relatives remained inside. There was a lot of weeping among them, while the groom's family tried to look appropriately sombre and understanding. Razia threw herself into Farhana's arms and bellowed, "Take good care of my daughter! She's been raised like a gentle flower. Promise me you'll treat her like your own flesh and blood!" Farhana awkwardly patted her back.

Then Razia looked deep into her doll's eyes with the eyelids that blinked. "You're leaving your parents' house and going to your real home. Take care of your husband and your mother-in-law, because I may have birthed you but she's your actual mother!"

"Yes," murmured the crowd of ten-year-olds. "A daughter is never her mother's forever. She must leave one day."

Farhana murmured, "You must be strong." She tried to take the doll but Razia held fast. Farhana tugged harder, but Razia was having too much fun playing the heartbroken mother. "Come on, Razia!" Farhana gasped. "Let GO!"

Razia only cried harder. "Let your daughter go to her own house now," Farhana said desperately. "She's married now. Let. Her. Go!" Farhana yanked so hard at the doll that Razia lost her grip and tumbled backwards into the rest of the "family" huddled behind her.

The groom's family jubilantly brought the bride to Farhana's house. They were holding the valima the next day. After that, Razia would take her doll back.

Farhana spent the entire evening playing with the doll that blinked. She told Khadija how much fun she'd had, how delicious the food was, and sang all the songs they had sung. She asked her mother what sort of food they were going to serve. Khadija sleepily replied they'd get something tasty from the corner café.

Muneer Ahmed was leaving for work when Khadija asked him for money. "Farhana has to have the valima today, and I thought I'd order food from the restaurant."

"I gave you money yesterday. Take some from that." He leaned over to tie his shoelaces.

Khadija chewed on the inside of her cheek and mumbled something.

Muneer glanced up distractedly. "What?"

"I said, it's all spent!"

Muneer was startled. "What? That was a whole month's expenses, Khadija! You spent it all in one day?" He shook his head in disbelief. "You're joking, right?"

"I'm not. I paid off all the bills yesterday," she said, ticking them off on her fingers. "I paid the milkman, the peanut man, the kulfi man, the rickshaw that takes me to Ammi's place…"

"What?" Muneer broke in with an incredulous gasp. "Your mother's house is at the end of the street! You need a rickshaw to go there? Are you mad?"

"I am sick!" Khadija shot back. "The sun's too hot. It gets to me. I feel faint. I tell you, I'm deathly sick!"

"No, you're not. You're lazy and spoilt, and you do this just to aggravate me. A bloody rickshaw for a ten-minute distance? How dare you throw my hard-earned money away like that?"

"Should I show you the doctor's prescriptions, then? You've seen the pills I have to take, the vile syrups they make me drink. The doctor knows I'm sick, that's why he gives me all those medicines. Are you saying the doctor is also mad?"

"He's a blood-sucking leech who's figured out that you're a stupid, ignorant woman and he can steal as much money from you as he wants. There's nothing wrong with you; he knows it and you know it. You like to believe you're sick because you want people to feel sorry for you, and you can't be happy unless you're taking medicines that cost half the earth and half the moon and make no difference to your 'illnesses'." He spat out the last word as though it were some insect that had flown into his mouth. "I've a good mind to beat that old quack to within an inch of his life."

Khadija snorted in derision. "Please, yes! Go and beat him up. He's just an old man, practically in his grave. You might even stand a chance to win!"

Muneer looked coldly at his wife, his thin frame quivering with anger. He turned to leave, barely noticing the three children who sat slack-jawed in a corner, watching the adults fight while their breakfast of bread and tea turned into a soggy mess.

"Are you giving me the money?" Khadija asked.

"No."

"Fine. There's a good father who doesn't care for his children. That daughter of yours," she pointed at Farhana, who wanted to vanish into her cup of tea, "has a dozen friends coming over for a valima feast and she has nothing with which to feed them. How is she to face them, I ask you! Why did you bring these children into the world if all you wanted was for the world to humiliate them?"

"Razia's father got food from a caterer," Farhana whispered to her brown toes poking out of slippers too small for her.

"Of course he did, child," Khadija crossed her arms across her chest. "Razia's father got lots of food because he wanted his daughter to walk out and look the world in the eye."

Muneer Ahmed studied his own daughter, the one who couldn't walk out and look the world in the eye. He looked towards Khadija. She raised her eyebrows and tossed him a smug, arch smile, but somehow, he didn't feel angry anymore. He was fed up. Fed up with this life where it was the same thing day in and day out, fed up with seeing his dreams crumble through no fault of his own. He was fed up with his wife, who made him feel like a worm in front of his own children, and he felt sorry for that scrawny child he had produced. Sorry, but nothing more. Poor child. Life stank and the sooner she learned about it the better. He walked out the door and closed it behind him.

Farhana swallowed the lump in her throat along with the lump of bread in her teacup. Her eyes welled with tears and she watched with interest as the salty drops plopped into the tan liquid. Khadija glanced at her, then impatiently grunted at the children to hurry or they would be late for school.

After school Farhana ran home as fast as she could to avoid the girls crowding around her, chattering with excitement about the party. Maybe she should ask for a miracle. Her mother said a child's prayers were always answered, so she prayed.

Please let Ammi have food for the valima.

Please.

Khadija lay on a string cot in the veranda. Safia Begum was visiting a cousin, a woman for whom Khadija had always felt a special hatred so instead of accompanying her mother, Khadija returned home and ate some peanuts. She tied the ratty blue chiffon scarf round her eyes and took a short nap.

When the children, not expecting her home, burst through the door like three small hurricanes, Khadija woke up and shouted at them to be quiet. They tiptoed into the veranda like scared little rabbits and sat down quietly in their little corner while Farhana got lunch. She filled a plastic plate with the potatoes Khadija had cooked and found some stale bread in a plastic bag. The children moved into a tight, cross-legged circle with the potatoes and bread in the centre and began to eat.

Khadija found she couldn't sleep anymore. She rolled over and watched her children scarfing down the meal with relish. "I saw your doll," she said to Farhana. "It's broken."

Farhana paused, a lump of potato wrapped in bread hovered in the air. Would Ammi get angry with her?

No. Khadija had another game in mind. "You know your doll is dead, don't you?"

"It's just his leg that fell off."

"Oh, you simple child." Khadija shook her head sadly. "It doesn't matter whether it's an arm or a leg or the head. Did you take your doll to the doctor? No. Just suppose your leg fell off and I didn't take you to the doctor. What would happen?"

Farhana prodded around her mouth with her tongue, dislodging a creamy lump of potato from her back teeth. She thought for a long moment. "I would die."

"Right. Your doll is dead as well, and you can't have a party when someone dies, especially when the party is because of him. Let's say you died after your leg fell off. Would you like it if I had a party?"

Farhana observed her mother warily. She didn't like all this talk of her supposed death. "What should I do?"

Khadija gently grasped her daughter by the shoulders and looked into her eyes. "You have to tell your friends that the groom is dead. It's Razia's fault. She married her evil doll to yours and killed him. Tell Razia to take her doll away. You don't want an evil witch in your home."

Farhana went inside where the doll sat on the shelf out of harm's way. She clambered on the bed and took it down.

Evil doll.

She bent the doll forward and its plastic eyelids with the thick black plastic lashes flew back. A cold lump formed in the pit of her stomach as she gazed into the doll's pale blue eyes. She looked out at where her mother sat watching her. Khadija touched her ears and frowned.

Evil.

They were coming by the tiny back lane. The moment she heard their laughter approach, she ran into the veranda and firmly threw the metal gate shut. She placed a chair by the door and stood on it, peering over the wall. The small group of girls turned the corner. They laughed and giggled, and shook their hands around so their bangles clinked. They wore bright clothes heavily stitched with gold and silver ribbon. They saw Farhana peering over the wall and waved. Farhana didn't wave back.

They tried to push the gate open, but the door wouldn't budge. "It's bolted, Farhana!" they called. "I know," she called back. The girls glanced at each other. "Aren't you going to open it?" asked Razia. "We've come for the valima. Let us in!"

"No!" Farhana shouted. "There will be no valima because you all killed my doll! Now you want to have a party? Have you no shame?"

The little, brightly coloured group gaped at her in astonishment. "Your doll didn't die!" they yelled. "You're cheating! You're not following the rules! We had the wedding, now you must have the valima!"

"No! All of you go home."

Razia stepped forward. "I know what you're trying to do!" she screamed. "You want to keep my doll! I want my doll back!"

"Your doll is evil!" Farhana shot back. "She's a witch. She killed her husband on the day of her wedding. Everyone knows that's what witches do." She pulled her arm back and flung the doll to the ground with all her might. It fell near a rotting cabbage. Razia yelped and scrambled to retrieve her precious toy, a process made more difficult since she also had to manage her silk dupatta, her large gold handbag and her oversized shoes.

"Go home, all of you! I hate you!" Farhana jumped off the chair and fled to find her mother. Khadija was propping the monthly supply of sugarcane, just delivered, in a shady spot against the wall. She selected a pale green length, snapped it neatly over her knee into foot-long pieces and gave one to Farhana, who tore off the shiny green bark with her teeth to get to the juicy, pale yellow pith inside. "I told them all to go home, just as you said. Razia thought I wanted to keep her doll but I never wanted that evil thing."

"Of course you didn't," Khadija stroked her daughter's hair soothingly with one hand, the other grasping her own piece of sugarcane. "I've a good mind to go and slap that little snip of a girl for breaking your doll, but isn't it nice, in a way? Now you can have a brand new doll that's far nicer than anything that spoilt brat could have."

Farhana got so excited she almost choked on the sugarcane. A brand new doll! Better than anything Razia—or anyone—had! She couldn't wait.

Muneer Ahmed came home that night and woke up his wife. "Get me something to eat. I'm going to wash and when I come back I want a hot meal on the table." He went to the small sink in the corner of the veranda and splashed cold water onto his face. Khadija silently watched as he dried his hands on the shred of towel hanging from a rusty nail.

"Well? What are you staring at me for? Get me some food!"

"Food?" Khadija crossed her arms across her chest and sneered. "Food? In case you didn't know, it costs money to cook food, to buy oil and meat and vegetables and if you can't give me any money then you can't expect a hot meal on the table."

Muneer groaned. "Khadija, I am so sick of this! I give you more than enough and you know it. I give you more in a month than that brother of yours can earn in fifty years! Stop telling me we don't have enough money because I don't earn enough; has it occurred to you that maybe it's because you don't know how to control yourself? Look at your brother's wife. I swear, that man earns a pittance and yet he has a savings account. His wife manages everything so well that his children go to a bloody private school! He can actually have someone over without being embarrassed that there's nothing to feed them. He has a bloody savings account, for heaven's sake!" Muneer was close to yelling now. "What have I got? Nothing!"

Khadija stared at him. Then, as though a pin had pricked a balloon, she felt herself deflate and sink to the ground. A wave of nausea swept through her, she looked at her husband in shock. Muneer, alarmed at the sight of her pale face, knelt down and clasped her hands tightly in his own. "Khadija, are you alright?" He felt afraid now. "Come, don't look like that. I'll be fine. I'll have something, someday. Just don't be like that!"

Khadija shook her head as though waking from a daze. "I don't believe it," she whispered. "I asked brother for some money today, and he flatly refused! He said he didn't have a rupee to spare, and now you tell me he has a savings account? A savings account! What kind of brother would lie to his own sister like that, when she needs him so much?" She pressed her hands to her eyes and slumped down.

Muneer felt his blood run cold in his veins. His body stiffened even as he held his wife in his arms. "You asked your brother for money?" his voice was dangerously low.

She raised her eyes and met Muneer's stony gaze. Her heartbreak over her brother's betrayal turned to defiance. "Yes, I asked my brother for money," she responded archly.

"Why?" It was not so much a question as a very quiet and dangerous demand.

"Because my husband doesn't earn enough to fulfil my needs or my children's needs!" she screamed in frustration. "You tell me to keep accounts? You compare me to Sadia Bhabi? My father was a judge, do you understand? The richest man in town! My mother never kept accounts and I wasn't brought up to pinch pennies! And you," she spat, "You with your vulgar fascination for saving money. I'd never have married you if I knew what a miser you were. And I'm not at all surprised that you worship that tramp who's sunk her claws into my brother and turned him against me, because she's a penny-pinching miser just like you!"

Muneer Ahmed wasn't exactly sure what transpired, but a moment later the tall and proud Khadija was sprawled on the floor, hand pressed to her left cheek, tears streaming down her face. Muneer inspected his hand. His wrist throbbed and the skin on his palm felt as though he'd scorched it on an open flame. Suddenly, he felt very tired. He stumbled to the kitchen, hunting in the dark for something to eat. There was some bread but nothing in the pot. Slowly, chewing on the hard, dry crust, he made his way to the door without seeing the three round little faces peering at him fearfully. Farhana, Ammara and Faraz clung to each other in a small little huddle and wondered what to do. Help Ammi? Stop Abbu? Go back to bed?

Something brushed against him. He swatted at it absently but it continued to buzz around him insistently. He flung it off his hand, walked out into the night and closed the door behind him.

Farhana watched the door slam shut, tears pricking the inside of her nose. She rubbed her hand, wishing Abbu hadn't slapped it away so hard. Khadija picked herself up, tied the blue chiffon dupatta round her forehead and was now stretched out on the string cot in the veranda. Ammara and Faraz stood around uncertainly. Farhana shooed them to bed and sat watching to make sure they didn't open their eyes. She thought about Razia's doll, the evil doll with the eyes that blinked. She thought about her own doll, the one with the broken leg and the orange hair and bit the inside of her lip. She'd thrown it away because Abbu was going to buy her a new one.

A month flew by but Muneer Ahmed didn't come home. Khadija took to her bed and Farhana looked after the children. Khadija found a pir who said her husband had run away because she didn't take good care of him. She called the pir a liar and a fake and found another. This one said her husband wanted to come home but he was lost. She asked how to bring him back. The pir ran his fingers through his snow white beard and said, "It will cost you."

"How much?"

He told her. She called him a liar and a fake and hunted for a third pir. This one asked for a somewhat reasonable amount, so she borrowed the money from her mother and paid him. He dipped a sharp stick into a bowl of yellow liquid that he claimed was saffron, wrote some words on a white china plate, then poured some water on it. The words dissolved in the water. She was supposed to drink this daily for a week and her husband would come home.

A month went by without any sign of Muneer Ahmed. The pir refused to return her money and Khadija came home and stewed. She debated telling her brother; he might bully the fake pir into giving her money back. Or he might stop the small amounts of cash he'd been giving her since Muneer disappeared.

She chose to keep quiet.

One day, Khadija and Safia Begum chanted the rosary while Khadija's children sat rocking on the floor, chanting prayers that would bring their father back. It had become their daily ritual now to come home from school, wash and pray for an hour before Khadija allowed them to go and play.

Khadija and her mother discussed the idea of holding a Quran Khwani to speed up Muneer's return. Sadia stood by the kitchen door, listening to them. "Certainly," she bitterly muttered to herself. "Hold the Quran Khwani to bring back the man you drove away and of course, I would love to cook all the food."

So deep were they in discussing the merits of biryani over pulao that they didn't hear Hamza come in. He handed his sister a letter postmarked Dhamanabad, India. Khadija drew out the single sheet of paper inside and read:

"My dear friend. I am aware of the pain I've caused you and certain members of your family. Forgive me, I had no choice. I've decided the new country isn't in my best interest and so I've returned to my family in India. I will not return. I will miss my children and I hope they will remember me fondly. I will try to send some money for their care. As for my wife, I'm sure she will be happier without me. If she wishes, I am willing to set her free. If other people are a nuisance, she may tell them I am dead."

There was a lot more to the letter that Khadija read out in a dull monotone, but Farhana didn't care. She quietly walked out of the room and no one saw her leave. She went home and crawled under the bed, scrabbling among the dust and dirt until she unearthed her doll.

The ugly thing looked even more hideous with the dust-balls caught in its orange, nylon hair. She inspected the doll's garishly painted eyes and the vacant socket that once contained a leg. She went into the veranda of the house, the doll clutched in her arms, drew back the bolts of the back gate. The lane was empty and a small pile of trash was neatly shoved against the wall two doors down. Farhana went and surveyed the heap of rotting vegetable peels and the flies swarming around it. The smell made her want to retch. She hovered for a moment, then bent down and quickly shoved the doll deep inside the pile of garbage. The head remained stubbornly visible, so she gave it a sharp kick in with her foot. Then she turned and ran to find her mother.

Photo Essay
Sign Your Name
Across My Heart

Attiq Uddin Ahmed

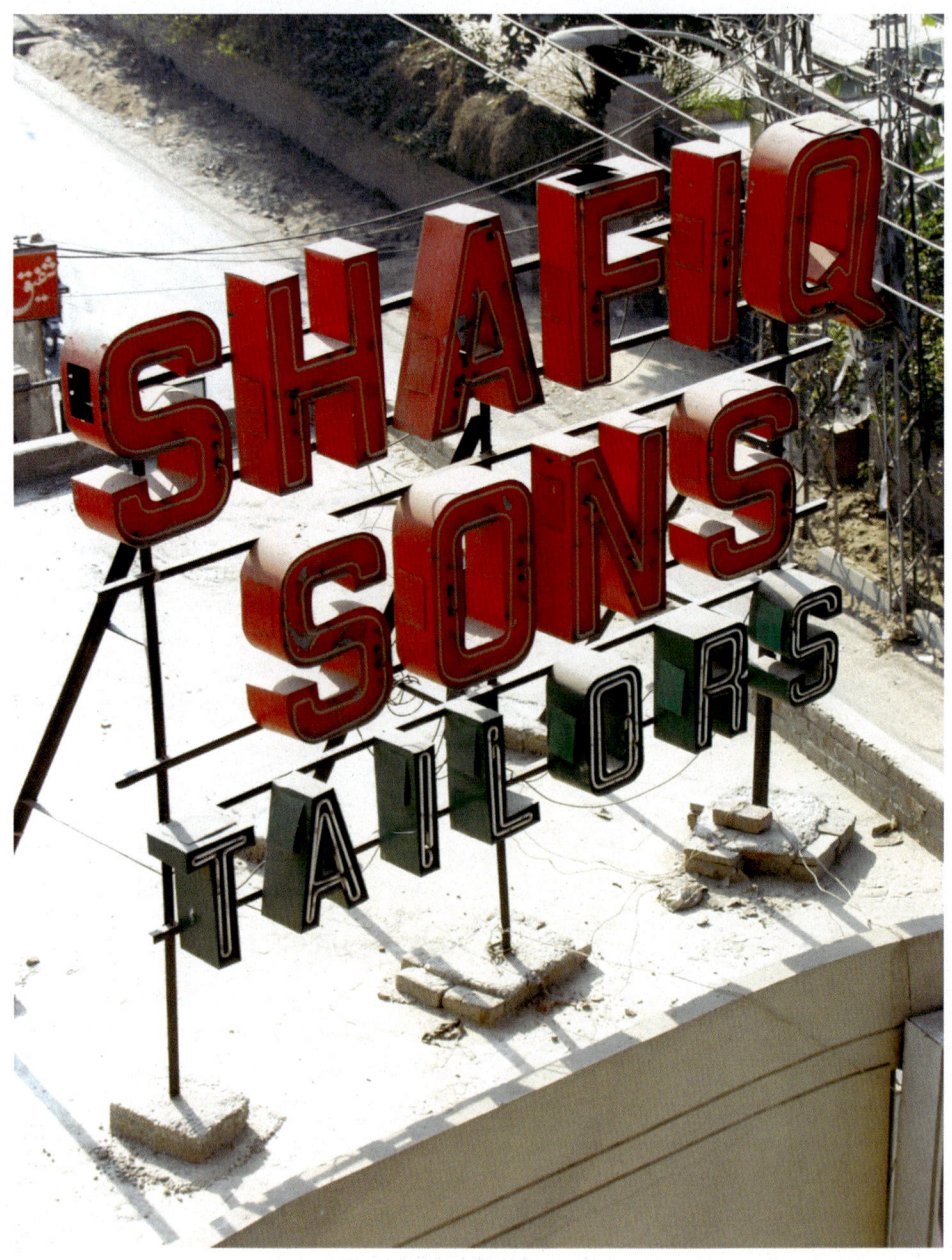

New Fiction
The Six-Fingered Man

Aziz A. Sheikh

Faisal tells me about the Six-Fingered Man on our way to school, just as we cross the frothing stream. Half-drowned rocks cut across the water; wobbly, slippery, velvety with moss. We skip from one to another, hoisting ourselves on the wet tops, twisting and lurching to keep balance. Faisal is good at this, confident. He keeps chatting all the while, his words scattering over the splashes of water. We're discussing the anomalies of human anatomy, natural or acquired. The Six-Fingered Man has an extra digit on his left hand, Faisal tells me, hence the sobriquet. He also tells me about the legless beggar and the one-eyed grocer. I know them both. The beggar crawls, crablike, all over the village alleys, pleading for food or money. Two smooth stubs of flesh for legs. And the grocer runs his little store in the village next to ours; for a few rupees he slips off the leather patch he wears, shows us the hollow of rumpled skin where his eye used to be. A splinter from an Indian mortar shell took it out, he claims. But Faisal says it was his wife. Faisal has his own opinions on things.

We talk of other freaks we know; the half-burned man, the boy with white hair and blanched skin and eyes that go blind in the sun. But I've never heard of this Six-Fingered Man. I'm curious.

"He works at Mai Kabootri's shrine," Faisal says, "he's been there a few months now. You know Kala Shah?"

I do. He's the head mystic at the shrine, known all over Kashmir. The chief spiritual guide-cum-faith healer-cum-miracle worker.

"The Six-Fingered Man is an apprentice of Kala Shah's, a junior mystic of sorts. They also call him Maula Peja. I've heard he's special: he can make magic with his hands."

Magic. I think of things emerging and disappearing, potent spells, deft fingers making miracles. I want to see this man, his six-digit hand.

"But he doesn't show off his gift," Faisal says, sensing my excitement. "It's a sacred thing, you know."

Faisal is resourceful; he knows things and people. The rest of the way to school I beseech him, promise him sweets and help with homework. I want to see those magical fingers at work.

"We'll see," he says.

At school everyone tussles for a place on the wooden bench, the only one we have. It's in poor shape—rickety, nail heads jutting out—but it's precious: the rest of the school sits on straw durries laid out on the hard, uneven ground. So the day begins with scuffles. Faisal whacks a big snotty-nosed boy out of contention—"You son of a pig!"—and subdues another with a kick. He secures enough space for both of us. I sit by his side, happy to be his friend.

Our schoolmaster, Mr. Akram, has a thick moustache and a chronic ailment up his nose that makes him go *sniff sniff* every time he says something. He sits in his chair in front of the class, sips his tea, flips through the morning paper, calls up boys from time to time and issues gruff orders. "Learn these adverbs! Tell me—*sniff, sniff*—what's nine times seven?" He spends an hour or two every day drilling kids. Faisal and I are in Class Four; we have to thoroughly memorise a lot of stuff. Multiplication tables, dates and names in history, rhymes. Mr. Akram canes us if we don't, or makes us pinch our ears and hop on our haunches. And when he's really pissed at someone he pulls them by the ears and drags them all around the schoolyard. That really hurts.

Today, after he's finished the morning paper and three cups of tea, Mr. Akram rouses himself from his chair and, with a stub of chalk, scribbles the date on our splintery, leprous blackboard: *June 9, 2000*. A hurried flourish, the trilogy of zeroes scrunched together. Satisfied, he sniffs and instructs us to open our Social Studies books at page 80 and begins his lesson. It's about Kashmir. Our beautiful home, he enthuses, our paradise, ruined by centuries of oppression and plunder and unrest. And even now, in this brand new millennium, the world just watches as we, the sons and daughters of Kashmir, continue to suffer. "Kashmir is burning!" he clamours. "Kashmir is burning!" we repeat aloud. I mouth the words but Kashmir is the last thing on my mind right now: I'm thinking of the six-fingered mystic. I see him sitting among spectres, communing with shadows, working his wizardry. He waves his hands and conjures a world of impossible colours, of varied wonders.

Mr. Akram points his cane my way and sniffs. "Usman! You're not listening. Stand up!"

I comply, heart pounding, legs going weak.

"Tell me, *sniff, sniff*, what was I saying."

Faisal nudges me, speaks in hurried whispers; atrocities, terror, freedom. I wrap a story around the words and tell it to Mr. Akram. "Kashmir is burning," I say with vehemence.

"Sit down, *sniff*, be more attentive."

"This is the season of frogs and fireflies," Faisal declares. We're sitting by the stream bank, building little mounds of mud. I'm cross at Faisal because he won't go to Mai Kabootri's this afternoon. He says it's far and there's a rain shower coming up, so maybe we'll go some other day. We spend the afternoon moulding clods of mud into imaginary things. It's breezy and cooler than most days, the sky all cloudy, the air scented with rain. This is the season of rains, monsoons. Rain beats the ground and drives frogs and fireflies and snakes and beetles out of their hideouts, Faisal says, so the creatures can wash their dirt off. "Do you know that snakes shed their skins during the rains?"

No I don't. I don't like snakes.

"They do. They take off their skins, grow new ones. And the skins grow new snakes."

We sit together a long while, building bigger, sturdier mud structures, fortresses of rival magical kingdoms. Battles are waged, arrows and cannonballs and mordant spells hurled at the enemy. By sundown everything is in ruins. There are no victors, no survivors.

It pours hard that night, a relentless shower buoyed by the wind, hissing, snapping at the mud and tin roofs of our village houses, gurgling down in rivulets. At home we put pots and pails under leaky spots in the ceiling; I spend the night listening to the sibilant downpour, the growl of thunder, the plop plop plop of water caught in buckets.

And also, in the distance the rattle of machine guns, the deep thud of mortars shot across the border. A heavy exchange tonight. Sometimes on such nights you can see huge flashes, flames snaking up the woods, the pyrotechnics of tracer rounds and incendiary rockets.

You can see Kashmir burning.

Mai Kabootri—the Pigeon Lady. She lived years and years ago, a noble, pious woman who lost her husband to some cause. Ghoondas invaded her house one night when she was all alone, threatened to taint her honour, her purity. She wept and wept and prayed and prayed: so hard that God transformed her into a pigeon and she flew off, never to be seen again.

Or so the legend goes.

Faisal has his own version, of course. He says the lady turned into a ferocious eagle, not a pigeon, and nipped and clawed the felons to death. He says her spirit lives on in the birds of the area.

I've been to her shrine a few times. It's a couple of villages away from ours, closer to the Indian border. A big, green dome, white pillars. The cenotaph inside was inscribed, legend has it, by saints and noblemen of yore, to honour the vanished lady. People come in droves; they drape the tomb with intricately embroidered sequined cloth sheets, string tinsel across her grave, shower it with rose and jasmine petals, sprinkle rosewater and perfumed oils around it, burn incense sticks and little oil lamps by the marble headstone, bow their heads and pray hard—for money, health, marriage, sons. They make pacts with Mai Kabootri: You urge Allah to grant me a boy, I'll feed a hundred hungry mouths. So there are plenty of hungry mouths around; shrivelled old beggars, cripples, kids in rags. The shrine's caretakers—bearded young men—dole out platefuls of dal and chappatis to the jostling crowd. And, in a nearby shack, Kala Shah hands out amulets to his devotees: holy verses scripted on bits of folded paper, strung around the neck or arms. To ward off disease, ill fate, the evil eye.

Faisal and I set off for the shrine on a Sunday afternoon. We cross the ring of wooded hills around our village, follow the rising, sloping, winding pathways that weave through clusters of cheer-pines and oaks and maples and converge eventually near a small bus stand on a country road. There we catch a ride to Mai Kabootri's. The road is cratered, sinuous. I feel my guts in my mouth with every bump, every heave and dip and twist in the way. I gulp down the nausea, stick my head out the window and gaze at distant snow-tipped peaks. Faisal pats my back. "There, there, easy does it." Everyone is watching us. It's embarrassing.

Once at the shrine we head straight for the mystic's shack, elbowing through the crowd. Faisal spots the Six-Fingered Man —"There! That's him! You see?"—sitting cross-legged at the entrance. He's quite a sight: scraggly, mustard-oiled hair—hennaed bright orange—tumbling to his shoulders; stark eyes rimmed with kohl; a florid, peppery beard; his face a mesh of lines. He looks menacing. A black cloak is draped over his shoulders, hiding his hands. There's a tin bowl in his lap, brimming with coins and rupee notes. These are offerings for Kala Shah, who is inside the shack prescribing charms and spiritual exercises for his clients. The Six-Fingered Man is merely ushering people in, collecting their donations. But he would succeed Kala Shah one day, Faisal tells me, once he completes his spiritual training. The man already has a reputation. He blesses people with his miraculous hand and heals them, dissipates their pain and sorrows. That's why they sometimes call him Maula Peja: God-sent. The God-sent Six-Fingered Man.

We want an audience with him alone, we decide. A chance to see magic. But how do we do that?

"Let's go talk to him," Faisal says. "I have an idea."

We squeeze through the thicket of devotees around the shack, wave and shout to catch Maula Peja's attention. We succeed, eventually: he nods our way.

"What do you want?"

Faisal does all the talking. He concocts a long-winded tale for the mystic, we two are brothers, our father has sent us for help; there's been a burglary in the house, lots of money and jewellery gone; we need the great Maula Peja, whose wisdom and powers are known all over Kashmir and beyond, to help us hunt down the thieves. We will, of course, pay for all expenses incurred in the effort, so please help us, Baba.

The pitch is convincing; there's a whine in Faisal's voice, a lilt of desperation. It's touching. The mystic tells us to wait while he sorts out the crowd, he'll talk to us afterwards.

We move away from the shack. From a nearby tea-stall Faisal fetches a bag of soggy, greasy chips that taste of kerosene oil. We eat them and wait.

Eventually the crowd thins out. The sun melts in brilliant, liquid colours and it starts to get dark. "We'll be late for home," I remind Faisal, "what will we tell our families?"

He just shrugs. "Don't worry," he says, "we spent the evening catching fireflies."

Maula Peja calls us when he's free, leads us down a dusty, litter-strewn path to another shack, a smaller, shabbier one. Mud walls and thatched roof. He pushes the splintering wooden door open and lets us in. He keeps his left hand tucked behind his cloak at all times, I note with dismay. His miracle is not for everyone to see.

It's dark inside the shack. He strikes a match, lights a kerosene lantern, ups the flame by twiddling the metal hoop at its side. An amber glow seeps through the sooty glass panels, a dull, flickering light. Shadows spill across the room. I look around. The room is austere; a pallet of rags on the floor, a hookah, a clay water pitcher lidded with a tin bowl, two squat straw stools by the far wall. There's a damp, warm smell of mud and sweat in the air along with kerosene fumes.

This is just what I had imagined: this shabby mud-shack, this light laced with shadows. This is where the mystic spins magic in my dreams.

Maula Peja drops on the pallet, tells us to pull up the straw stools. His voice is grainy, cardamom on his breath.

"You want me to identify the burglars. It will be done. Allah is most benevolent! The world will bare its secrets to you. You'll see the thieves' faces shining on your thumbnails. You'll see the whole burglary enacted! Allah is most powerful!"

He lights his hookah, stirs the contents of its cup—smouldering ash, half-burnt herb leaves, crumbs of dried buffalo dung—and draws a huge swig from the wooden pipe. Water bubbles at the base of the hookah, *gurh gurh gurh*. Smoke whorls out of the man's mouth and nostrils. The smell is sharp, ticklish.

"So, who wants to spot the thieves?"

Faisal and I consult in whispers. I'm a bit scared—there are no thieves, won't the mystic find out? What then? But I don't want to miss this chance. This is magic, burglars or no burglars. I volunteer.

Maula Peja instructs me to come closer. He produces a small glass bottle from under his pillow and places it before him. This, he announces, is a precious oil, culled from the juices of rare herbs and killer snakes and scorpions. He uncorks the bottle and begins his incantations. Verses and prayers hummed in a fervent tenor. A flurry of words. He pauses every now and then to gulp smoke from the hookah and blow it my way. The smoke hangs like mist around me, spiralling into wispy shapes, prickling my skin, my thoughts. I see ancient veiled women, rolling hills, moths in flight. Fantastical beasts poised for attack. I see the spirit of Mai Kabootri wafting from her tomb.

Faisal nudges me. "Are you okay?"

I can barely see him, smoke and shadows shifting between us. He seems far away, a memory from another life. I nod yes, I'm fine.

Maula Peja's mantras grow louder, more passionate. He rocks back and forth with every syllable, jerking his head to the cadence of sacred words, his tresses flying. When he finishes, he's all sweaty and breathless. "Your right hand," he demands.

I comply. He holds my hand in his right, shrugs off the cloak from his shoulders. There! I see the sixth digit for the first time. An extra pinkie, curled wormlike against its twin. But there's nothing magical about it: it's deformed, he can't even move it.

He tips the glass bottle, collects some oil in his palm and begins rubbing it over my hand: my fingers, palm, wrist: he strokes and kneads each part. Pulling my hand closer, he dabs some oil on my thumbnail. "This hand is blessed," he says, and presses his lips on my wrist. His warm wet breath is ticklish on my skin, I start giggling. He smiles and strokes my cheek.

"Sweet child." His teeth are crooked and stained. "Here, taste this," he offers me his hookah. "You'll feel good."

Faisal lets out a little squeal. "Oy Usman! I see them! The burglars. Right there on your thumbnail. Can't you see?"

I pull my hand away from the mystic, stare hard at the thumbnail. Nothing there but glistening oil.

"Thank you Baba," Faisal cries, "we've seen the goons' faces, very clearly. We have to leave now," he grabs my arm, "it's getting late. Father must be worried." He jerks my hand. "Let's go!"

I'm confused. I haven't seen any magic yet, I want to stay. But Faisal keeps tugging at me.

The mystic glares at us. "Wait! *This* boy was supposed to glimpse the burglary. You can't leave just yet."

But Faisal repeats "Thank you, thank you Baba", and pulls me away. He yanks open the door of the shack and drags me into the fading twilight. "Come on!" he shouts as we scramble towards the shrine. I glance back and see the Six-Fingered Man standing outside his shack, scowling, the black cloak back on his shoulders like a bat's wings. "Bastards!" he yells. "Sons of filthy dogs!"

I sit dazed through the bus ride back home. The world shifts and twirls around me, grotesque, jarring. My innards keep churning till I can't hold back anymore and puke by the window, twice, splattering the bus's rexine interiors and its ornately painted hull. The driver catches this in rear view and yells at me. "Oy! Stop, boy! Who'll clean this mess? Your mother?"

"Why should she," Faisal snaps. "What good is your wife?"

This sparks a big fight and we're forced off the bus. Fortunately we're close to our stop, so we walk. Faisal is all hot and red, mad at the bus driver—"Son of a pimp!"—and at me because I didn't counter the mystic's advances. He thinks that the man was drugging me, planning to do bad things to me. I should have resisted.

But I don't know. Maybe he was just making magic.

Night falls quickly around us, star-sequinned dark. We climb the pathways in the hills, groping, taking cautious steps. Faisal leads, he's a better climber. He hands me some rocks. "For the jackals. Aim at the head."

A pale half-moon rises in the far edge of the sky, a tilted bowl, its glow muffled by cottony clouds. We pause for a while, waiting for the moon to climb higher, listening to the night's music. Crickets, frogs, owls, brooks purling down rocky slopes, dogs and jackals howling. The place, drenched in night, is scary. I expect wandering ghosts and ghouls of all sorts to pounce on us any moment.

"Look," Faisal points to a shrub on my left. "Look at that!"

I do, heart racing. Tiny blue jewels in the bushes: pulsing, wiggling lights.

"Our excuse," Faisal says. "Let's catch some."

We go home with fireflies blinking in our pockets.

My dreams that night are jumbled phantasmagorias. I see Mr. Akram twirling his moustache. "Today, *sniff*, *sniff*, I teach you magic." Smoke swirls around his words and when it clears he is the Twelve-Fingered mystic, snarling insults and curses at me. He fetters me with wicked spells, drags me all around the schoolyard. He waves his evil hand and I slump to the ground, my legs gone. I'm the legless beggar! I see my grotesque stumps and start wailing, wailing, begging for help. But I'm snagged in his curse forever.

I wake up gasping, feeling like I have grains of sand in my throat. My ears are filled with the din at the border miles away. Crack! Thud! Boom! A raging beat, louder than on most nights. I gaze outside the window and see flames lapping up the pines in No-Man's Land, whipped by a strong breeze, raying out into the surrounding knolls and beyond. I see mortars whistling across the sky, crashing on either side of the border. Whoosh, BOOM!

The explosions peter out near dawn; I drift to sleep around that time, with the blush of morning in the horizon, muezzins calling for prayers in euphonious tones. I sleep soundly, without dreams.

Faisal has news for me when we meet, later that morning, on our way to school. He's all excited. "You heard? Mai Kabootri's shrine got bombed! A stray mortar from across the border, or maybe someone planted something. They're investigating."

This is big news. I tell Faisal that we have to go see.

So we play hooky. We catch a ride to the shrine but the bus is stopped a couple of miles short by a band of soldiers. Camouflage fatigues, fierce faces. We can't go any further, we're told, the area has been cordoned off. The army is sorting things out, helping the injured. No, no one was killed; things are under control. But the shrine is off limits for now. Turn back!

Faisal and I hop off the bus. He has an idea.

We clamber up a grassy ridge, shielded by brush and shaggy pines. Faisal leads me to a cliff, a safe vantage point.

The shrine below is a mess, roof caved in, walls blown out, rubble everywhere. Soldiers and policemen sifting through the wreckage, marshalling knots of shocked people away. We see blood, chunks of flesh. "People definitely got killed," Faisal mumbles. "That soldier was lying."

I try to make out the mystics' shacks; there's too much rubble, too many people. "What do you think happened to Maula Peja?" I ask Faisal.

"Don't know. Can't tell from here. Maybe he got injured, they took him away. The shrine's had it anyway; they'll have to build a new one."

We gaze quietly at the ruins. "See that?" Faisal points to a massive buzzard circling and swooping in the air, keening, fluttering its enormous wings.

"What?"

"Mai Kabootri. She is pissed."

We spend the rest of the day lazing by the stream bank, chatting, watching earthworms and beetles ploughing the mud. "Have you heard about the man with mottled skin?" Faisal asks.

No, I haven't.

"He has these weird blotches all over his body, ugly pink-purple spots. They say someone cursed him: black magic."

"Really, is that possible?"

He scoops up an earthworm from the mud, lets it curl around his thumb. "Nah! Sounds like a silly old tale."

Archive
Notes from
The Reluctant
Fundamentalist

Mohsin Hamid

JANNISARY LOVE, ANOTATED

THE STORY OF A YOUNG PAKISTANI CONSULTANT, MAJNOO, WHO FALLS IN LOVE WITH AN ITALIAN WOMAN, FRANCESCA, AND PURSUES HER THROUGH A WILD ROMANCE THAT ENDS IN FRIENDSHIP.[1]

1. WITH AN ANALYSIS BY A MEMBER OF THE JANNISARY CORP., AN ORGANIZATION THAT MONITORS THE ACTIVITIES OF MUSLIMS WORKING IN THE WEST

NAMES: MAJNOO (LOVER WAS LAILA)
         FRANCESCA (LOVER WAS PAULO)
         COMMENTATOR — AN ANAGRAM?

IDEAS: JANNISARY CONCEPT REVERSED —
         YOUNG MUSLIM WHO SUPPORTS THE
         WESTERN EMPIRE.

THE MANUSCRIPT: Q → HOW DOES THE ANNOTATOR COME TO ANNOTATE? BORGESIAN SOLUTION?
IS THE BOOK A ROMANCE ALREADY IN EXISTENCE,
AN AUTOBIOGRAPHICAL ACCOUNT BY THE PROTAGONIST (MAJNOO)

New Fiction
Ruth and Richard

Madiha Sattar

Ruth woke to the nauseating whiff of eggs frying in butter. It was Sunday, and like every other Sunday she could remember, Richard had been banging about in the kitchen for their lone frying pan before she had rubbed her eyes, got out of bed and gone down the stairs to the neighbourhood patisserie where Claude behind the counter would hand her a skim Splenda cappuccino and pain au chocolat as if they were French porn. Then it was back up to the apartment, picking up the *Times* along the way. For the weekly breakfast routine that was, by now, well-rehearsed, she started with the Style and Arts sections in the chair by the window that looked north up Avenue A; he ate sunny-side-ups and toast with the *Week in Review* and his back to the street. From here he commanded a view of the faded one-bedroom they had not yet managed to buy, that object most other Manhattan couples they knew seemed to have acquired several years ago.

Ruth Mohammad, nee Miller, failed novelist, one-time *Paris Review* intern and sometime tween romance ghostwriter, and her husband Richard, political-socio-cultural commentator on a wide and vague range of Pakistan-related topics, had settled into a state of angst-ridden inertia. There was no time, between sustaining dead-end careers, developing real estate strategies and shopping for Humboldt Fog, to go through the motions of divorce, dating and remarriage.

They had not always been East Villagers. Before they turned twenty-six, decided to believe in love and moved to 10th Street, Richard would climb five long flights to her tenement-building studio on the fringes of Soho, a magical place where they had soaked in the beautiful people and the foreign accents, the shiny promise of never-ending youth and the belief that as long as there was stylishly chopped hair and sushi and champagne and Parliaments and cocaine and one was thin and tall and beautiful, or at least thin and good looking, one could continue to believe that living in this city was bearable, or at least doable. Some of these crutches had diminished, but none had disappeared. There was still the rare line done at the after party for a book launch, the occasional briefly exhilarating and ultimately inconclusive one-night stand with Claude or Richard's editor Judy, and the more frequent cigarette when they allowed smoking in the apartment in an unspoken hankering for the edge life used to have.

They discussed, briefly, their schedules for the week: the Santos' dinner party on Monday, her colleague's book launch at Housing Works on Wednesday, drinks with his agency tonight. She would probably stay away from this last event, choosing, as always, not to suffer his agent's bumbling efforts to flirt with him while pretending not to. Ruth might have been able to muster jealousy if Zainab had only been twenty-six and beautiful. As it was, the younger woman also offered something else she never could—a taste of Richard's lost heritage (how she despised that word!)—and she was glad to have the burden of his nostalgia taken off her hands.

She found it more than mildly irritating, his Sunday performance with the eggs. Toast two slices of white bread till almond-brown. Painstakingly slice off crusts; set aside. Slide spoonful of room-temperature butter into cast iron skillet over flame neurotically adjusted to perfect heat. Slather Kraft cream cheese (rich, velvety international kind purchased from Agha's in Karachi, never chalky American plastic tub version) onto toast with butter knife. Tap two eggs elegantly against edge of diminutive Manhattan kitchen counter; break tenderly into butter. Fry till edges of whites curl up and grow golden brown. Inhale glorious scent deeply. Slice whites off; set aside. Place each glistening, trembling yolk on bed of toast. Close eyes; bite lustily; savour burst of liquid yolk swirling into cream cheese, settling into grooves in bread, flowing into mouth and dripping onto plate. When done, dip toast crusts and egg whites into pool of remaining yolk; consume slowly to delay impending end of joyful breakfast. Coax with tongue last bits of meal out of corners of mouth and furrows of teeth. Look more satisfied than after occasional sex with wife.

The instinct behind this ritual was, to her, pathetically obvious. Richard was seven years old again at his grandparents' casual dining table for ten in Karachi, dangling his legs over the edges of a Danish mid-century chair upholstered in orange-gold Girard checkers, following his grandfather step by step in this elaborate culinary rite of a bonding exercise. Every Eggs Benedict he had ever consumed in New York was a sensible-world, English-muffined shadow of the Ideal Breakfast, or, more precisely, the Ideal Life. As if he could have lived in Pakistan, even with a Pakistani wife. Richard had at some point during their seventeen years of marriage started to imply, with every other word and action, that he was trapped in five hundred square feet of living space and a journalistic rat race because of Ruth, once the female version of his personality and the everything he would never find in anyone else. As if, at forty-three, Karachi would still be warm milk with Ovaltine after breakfast and he would spoon out the moist chocolate powder clinging to the bottom of his glass before handing it back to the nanny standing by to receive it. As if, every winter, Beatrice Mohammad would still be alive to ignore her son chasing around their enormous lawn the imported Pekingese who were in constant danger of dying from heart attacks. As if, every summer, Haroon Mohammad would still have the faculties to play chess and drink mango milkshakes with his son while his wife recovered from Pakistan back home in South Ken.

It was during their routine walk in Tompkins Square Park later that afternoon that, from boredom or habit, Ruth decided she was going to pick the scab.

"I assume Zainab will be at drinks tonight?"

"I suppose so."

"I suppose I should stay away then."

"What does that mean?"

"It means it would bore me to weeping to hear about her latest trip home. The scent of the motherland. Bihari kababs etc."

"She hasn't been back to Karachi since the last time you met her."

"That won't help her snare the Ivy-educated Pakistani industrialist she should probably be looking for."

"She has Pakistani friends here."

"She's too career-focused. Maybe what she needs is a gora-Paki who only thinks he's Paki. Someone like you."

"I'm unavailable, in case you hadn't noticed. Did you read the Dining section today? Brian's opening a new bar in Long Island City. The community board here denied him that space around the corner."

"The one I want to open a cafe in? You could host Pakistani authors for their New York book readings. They're touring through in droves now."

"And you would fund this how?"

"Get one of our friends to invest. Postcolonial fiction with a side of chai and paan. We'll bring over all those intellectual types you seem to know out there. All eleven of them."

"You keep insisting I still have friends at home. I only used to. Look at Benita today—I think she finally got her moustache waxed."

Ruth followed his gaze to the empanada shack across the street and watched as the seventy-two-year-old owner of the neighbourhood institution attacked her sweaty dough with a rolling pin. Ham and mozzarella wafted over, tinged with old grease and pineapple. Richard waved and smiled broadly. She felt sick.

It was almost exactly the same disgust she felt when, at the agency event later that night, Ruth watched Richard whispering into the ear of a teenaged cocktail waitress as if they were just another mid-life-crisis couple in a marriage that was only coming undone in the standard way. She had fixed herself in one corner of the wood-and-glass loft that was suspended like a display case in the Manhattan sky, and by the standards of these affairs she was having a decent enough conversation, reminiscing with an old editor from the *Review* and with Rachel who had grown up on her block in Queens and lived in her hallway at Yale. Mostly, though, she was wondering why she had allowed herself to come here at all. She had made three new acquaintances already, but they were the usual literary suspects with a new set of names; she "had already met them, always," Ruth remembered from Joan Didion's essay about leaving New York, before admitting that fleeing the city might rescue her marriage but would leave her entirely dependent on it.

Richard was doing his rounds now, no doubt avoiding questions about her, his current projects, and Pakistan. As always, in her presence, he was also skirting around Zainab. Ruth watched her, little black dress with long black hair, from a distance.

He liked to guess, when suffering through these agency gatherings, how many other clients were failing as precipitously as he. Was the columnist across the table also wondering which of them earned more per piece? He sipped his St Germain cocktail, concentrated, mentally narrowed his eyes. Barney's—that's where he had seen her spectacles, the ones he hadn't been able to justify buying because they had a higher price tag than the average rate of a Richard Mohammad op-ed. The ones this woman—he couldn't even recall her name—could clearly afford.

He looked around for the waitress he had shared a cigarette with on the fire escape in the back by the kitchen, where he had tried to determine if her particular shade of brown could possibly be considered blonde. She was an NYU philosophy student, Spanish, about his height in heels—only average for a woman in Manhattan—but with curves just the right amount of curved, a perfect B cup, green eyes, an olive tan, and the full European eyebrows that finally led him to suspend the knowledge that his wife was around. That, and Richard's sense that she was impressed enough by his credentials to give up half an hour of tips to sneak upstairs with him.

They served him well socially, these past achievements. The brief television appearances during war-on-terror news broadcasts began soon after 9/11, when he was a writer at a not particularly well-known international affairs magazine, but it didn't take long for him to be crowned an expert on any number of topics having to do with Pakistan and the Taliban. Eventually there had been a handful of *Foreign Policy* columns, a few *Times* op-eds, and a book, but it was this last effort, shot down by critics and especially by Pakistani journalists—the "literary Taliban," as Ruth described them until she saw he didn't find it amusing—that got in the way of his rapidly growing importance. Another type of hack would have trudged on, but as it was, the distance between a boy on a Danish chair in a Bath Island drawing room and the suicide-bombing youth of southern Punjab had been growing too vast to ignore, and the book's reception only fed into Richard's fears of being unqualified to comment on the things Americans wanted him to comment on.

There the waitress was, in the corner flirting with Jason Dowde, film critic and frequent contributor to *Vanity Fair* on issues of great cultural import, as she served him a Tom Collins. It washed over Richard again, then, that sordid sense of repetition that Manhattan nightlife humiliates one with every now and again. Nereida would go home with Dowde, who had not developed a bald spot in the middle of his hair, who could stay up all night and write when the beast possessed him, who did not have to share his breakfast table every Sunday and his bed every night with a woman he no longer had anything to say to, a woman who was jealous of an entire country three continents and two decades away. Dowde, who did not have to fudge the timeline of his achievements, was going to sample the mind and matter of a woman who would not lie there resenting Australia while he made love to her.

Behind them, on the flat screen mounted on the wall, Richard spotted women in black shrouds shuffling through dusty streets under the gaze of rugged tribesmen with rocket launchers slung over their shoulders like suit jackets. Shopkeepers in skullcaps stared into the camera in the winding alleyways of a bazaar in Mingora or Swabi or Peshawar. The screen switched to heart-strings shots of filthy children fighting for food and rolling around in the dust of a camp for families displaced by the military operation in Swat. It was, more than anything else, exhausting: the constant media flip book of cartoon-caricatures that provoked an anger he had eventually grown tired of articulating; the tedious expectation of Manhattan's most cosmopolitan that he would be able to untangle and explain the mess of it all. What they didn't understand was the thing he didn't want to say, that his own golden Karachi was just as unreal as CNN's Peshawar.

He remembered again, then, writing exams on Eliot, Larkin and Blake, verses of Urdu poetry about eyes and wine and loss, his grandmother running off to discos in her scandalous little numbers, and, later, even after the discos had gone underground, his ambitious girlfriends taking off to the best colleges in the world, his aunt who ran the State Bank, her husband who showed her off. He thought of art galleries and theatre and guilty mornings after.

This time, though, CNN was offering more than just a photo montage of northwestern Pakistan with Amanpour and Zakaria soundbites about the channel's global sensibility. This time there had been some big bomb that had killed more families than usual somewhere crowded in some godforsaken town of that province that believed in Allah. Richard watched from a distance as the concerned crowd gathered around Zainab, cocktails in hand, sympathies in place, Ivy League training immediately focused on asking her the relevant questions. Seventy dead, CNN announced. The death toll is expected to rise as more information becomes available. A Taliban commander has claimed responsibility. The suicide bomber was fifteen years old. Hospitals are strained. Pakistan's leaders are expressing grief and keeping bereft families in their thoughts and prayers at this difficult time. The Indian Prime Minister offers his condolences. Pakistan is the epicentre of militant Islam. The world is united with it in its war against terror.

"Trust everyone at home alright?"

It was Dowde, sans sophomore but with fresh drink in hand, dressed in premium denim and a black shirt entirely too fitted for his age and buttoned a button less than it should be.

"My family are all in Karachi, actually."

"Still, it must be hard to live in fear of a bomb going off while you're driving to the grocery to buy milk and eggs."

"Wouldn't know. I haven't lived there in more than two decades."

"But you visit often. And you must be worried about your folks."

"Their lives are not really..." Richard trailed off. "Like that."

"They have money, I get it. The rich and the fucked, that's pretty much how it breaks down across the developing world. The wealthier you are, the less likely you are to get killed."

"You're absolutely right. So I wouldn't ask me. I'd ask your average Karachiite, a creature that apparently exists. But somehow they can never find him to put him on TV."

"There's a story there, you know. Pakistan human interest, the faces and places behind the story, the personal in the political, that sort of thing. I should try it myself—maybe something about the possibilities for producing and consuming art in a conflict zone that also happens to be poor and sexist and Islamist. D'you think your family would have me?"

"I'm sure they'd like that. But I don't know if you'll find any poor sexist Islamists at the house."

"Not sure I'm ready for the real Pakistan anyway, so that's probably for the best. I hear the women are rather attractive?"

"I suppose so. My wife's not from there, so, again, not best person to speak to. Would you excuse me, Jason?. I think I'm going to step out for some air..."

"Are you sure? This situation looks serious."

Richard would have ignored the courtesy update and moved outside to escape the oppressive fretting around him if it wasn't for Zainab, who from the corner of his eye he saw crumpling onto a sofa as people around her dutifully relayed to no one in particular that she was dialling relatives in Karachi. He was confused for a moment, not realising why she was calling his city, the place where, for him, Pakistan took place all at once, the place one would call if one had to call anyone in the country. But there was a chorus of people asking others to fetch her water, turn down the television, make space on the couch, give her some air, her father might be dead, and although asking anyone was not something he could bear to do, he found himself listening to discover that the bomb in some godforsaken town had been a bomb in Karachi, and that the building Zainab's father worked in had leaned, until twenty minutes ago, against the one that had been blown to bits.

Her call failed to go through yet again, and when she began to scan the room he knew she was looking for him. He wondered whether to meet her eyes and confirm all the convenient explanations—Richard the failed opinion-maker trying to salvage himself through an affair with a pretty young agent, and, for Ruth, Richard the unfaithful husband who had dumped her for a woman able to conjure up a mythical past. Behind him, he knew, she would be stoically watching the aftermath of yet another bomb that had widened the space between them.

He stepped out onto the terrace and inhaled the hot, sharp Manhattan air, as pungent as Karachi on a summer day, but smelling more of rotting garbage than exhaust fumes. And there it was, what he had come out here looking for, rising magnificently over the loft—the Chrysler Building, pure, clean, and clarifying, like the string of diamonds fiery around Mum's pale neck the December nights she would go dancing at the Palace Hotel, now site of the Sheraton, where 11 Frenchmen and 2 Pakistanis died in a car bomb in 2002, across the street from the Pearl Continental where he had had sashimi with Sauvignon Blanc in 2008, a couple of miles from the barricaded US embassy but also from the Sind Club, where in 2006 he had met that timid young woman whose husband was denied membership because her hijab made the swimming pool lot uncomfortable, where in 2003 he had played tennis with that brash young lawyer with a Bachelor's in gender studies from Wellesley and a law degree from Cambridge.

In actual fact, nothing was clear but the glossy white beauty rising up in front of him.

RABBIT RAP

Text by Musharraf Ali Farooqi | Drawings and lyrics by Michelle Farooqi

CHAPTER 1

*Which is really only an excerpt from THE LAPIN DYSTOPIA,
one of the late Professor Smulflem Noks's better known works,
and quoted here for the admirable way
in which it delineates the background of this narrative*

"The post-predatorial age was ushered in by the pesticide UB-NEXT. Originally meant to ward-off crop-eating weevils, it really seemed aimed for the furry carnivores. All of them who came in contact with it died from a mysterious skin disorder. Organic farmers and animal rights groups protested the use of UB-NEXT, but the damage had already been done. Within a matter of months the pesticide wiped out entire popula-tions of badgers, coyotes, foxes, stoats, wolves, wolverines and ferrets."

"The survivors disappeared deep underground into the multi-story garbage disposal dungeons."

"The greatest beneficiaries of UB-NEXT were the rabbits. It had no adverse effect on them: Though furry they were not carnivores. Moreover, the rabbits were the biggest farm-owners. The pesticide not only eliminated the weevil threat, it rid the rabbits of their main predators as well."

"Even after the effects of UB-NEXT were known, the board members of the Lapin Alliance for Progressive Sowing Endeavors (L.A.P.S.E.) refused to curtail its use."

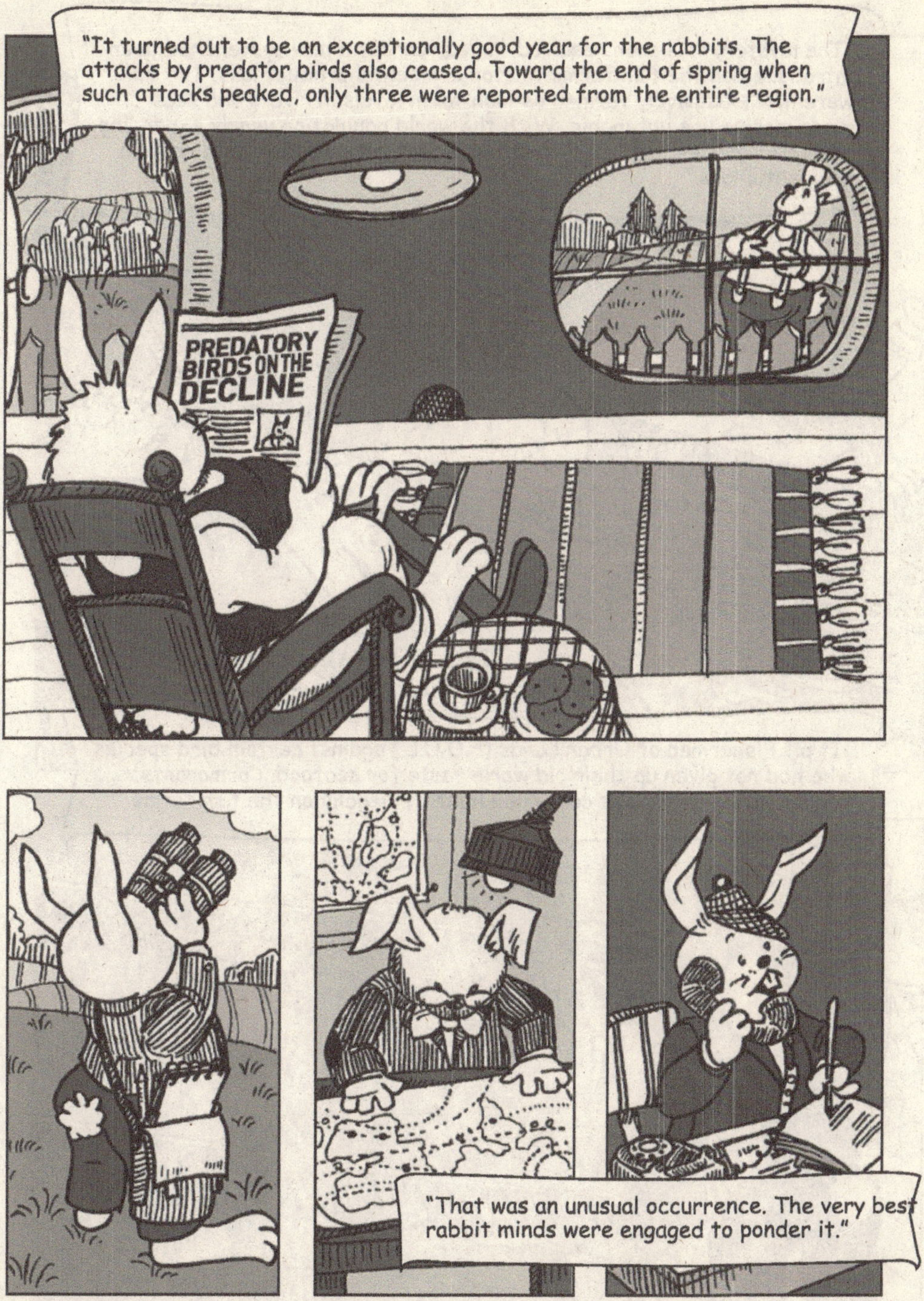

"It turned out to be an exceptionally good year for the rabbits. The attacks by predator birds also ceased. Toward the end of spring when such attacks peaked, only three were reported from the entire region."

"That was an unusual occurrence. The very best rabbit minds were engaged to ponder it."

"The mystery was soon resolved. A year earlier a new system had been introduced on the fish farms to stop accidental product loss. The fish were now exclusively farmed as high toxin levels in rivers and seas made marine life untenable. With the world population yearly expanding to new extremes, every fish counted. Great care was taken to contain accidental loss."

"It pit Fishermen of Urban Lands (F.O.U.L.) against certain bird species who had not given up their old world taste for seafood. Cormorants, eagles, kites, and hawks continued hunting illegally on the fish farms."

SECURITY

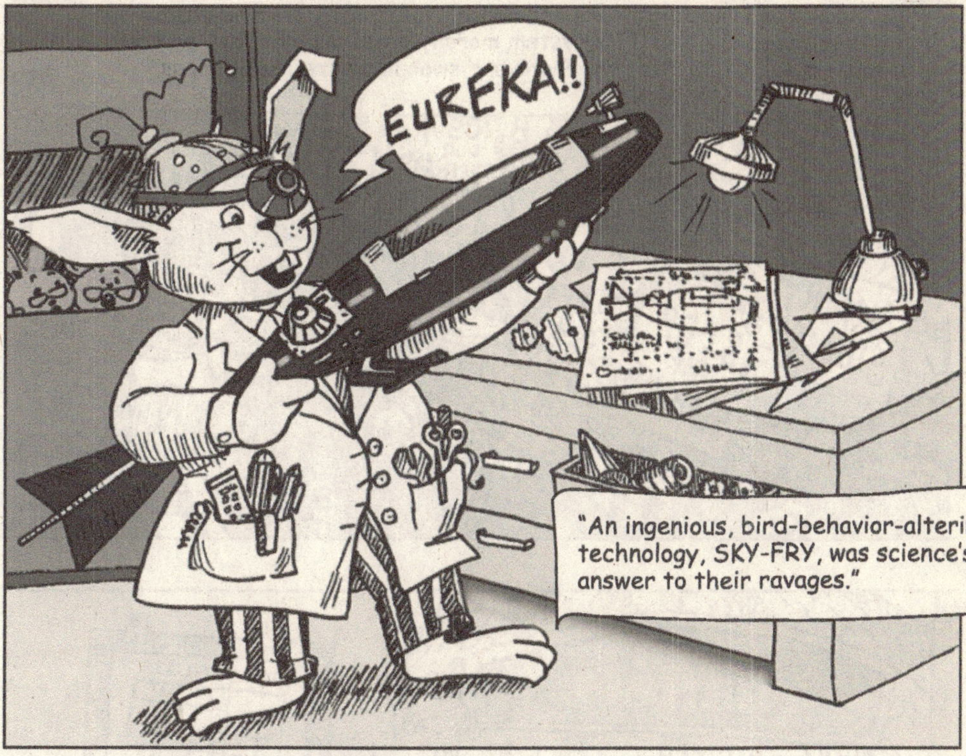

"An ingenious, bird-behavior-altering technology, SKY-FRY, was science's answer to their ravages."

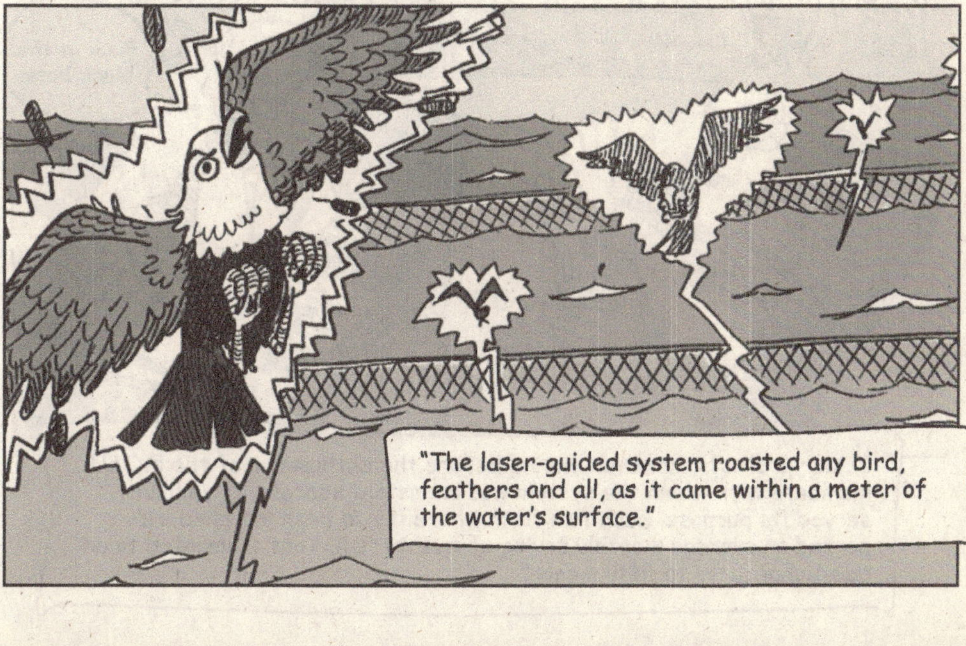

"The laser-guided system roasted any bird, feathers and all, as it came within a meter of the water's surface."

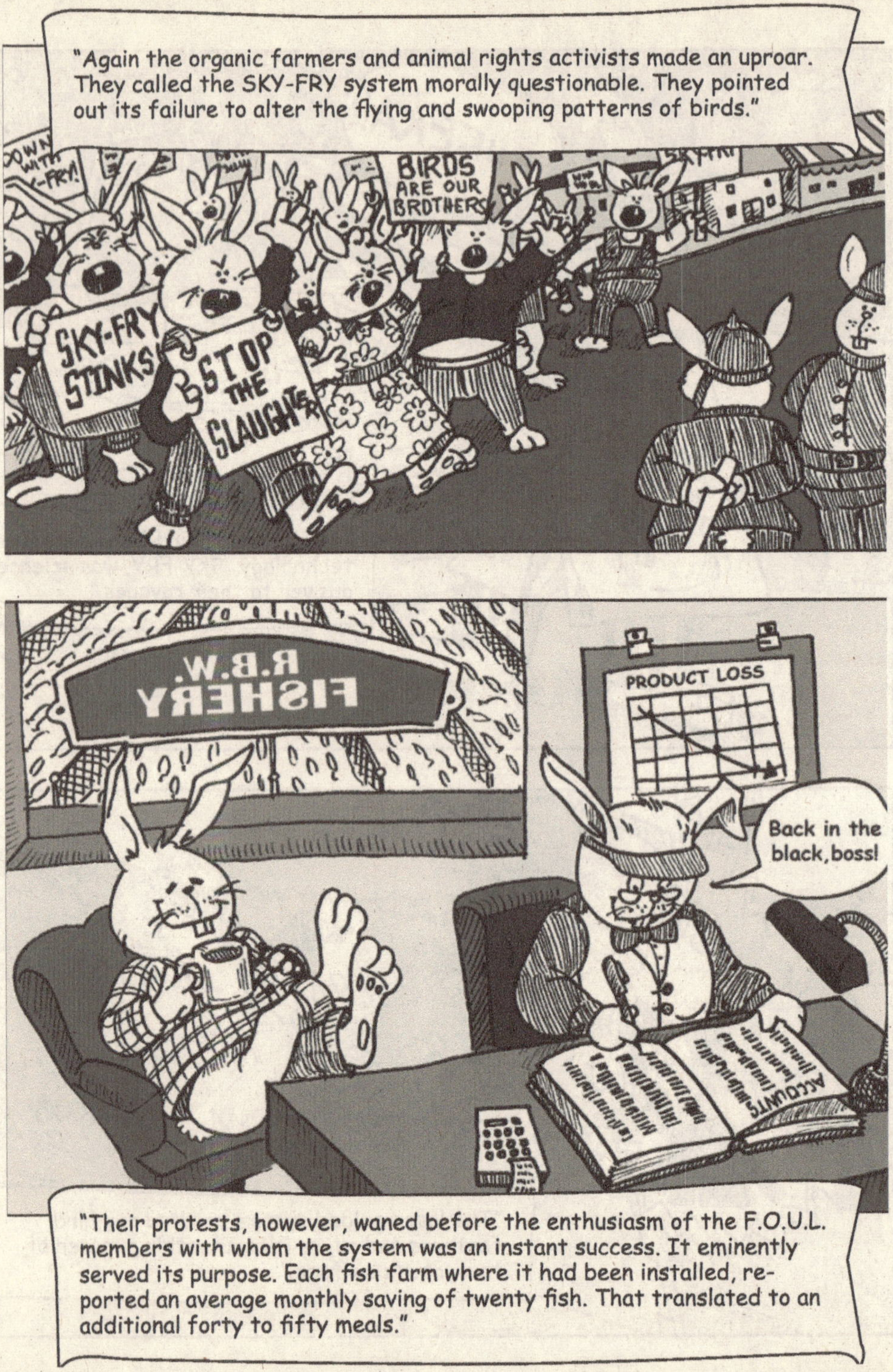

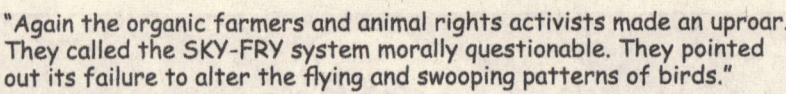

"Again the organic farmers and animal rights activists made an uproar. They called the SKY-FRY system morally questionable. They pointed out its failure to alter the flying and swooping patterns of birds."

"Their protests, however, waned before the enthusiasm of the F.O.U.L. members with whom the system was an instant success. It eminently served its purpose. Each fish farm where it had been installed, reported an average monthly saving of twenty fish. That translated to an additional forty to fifty meals."

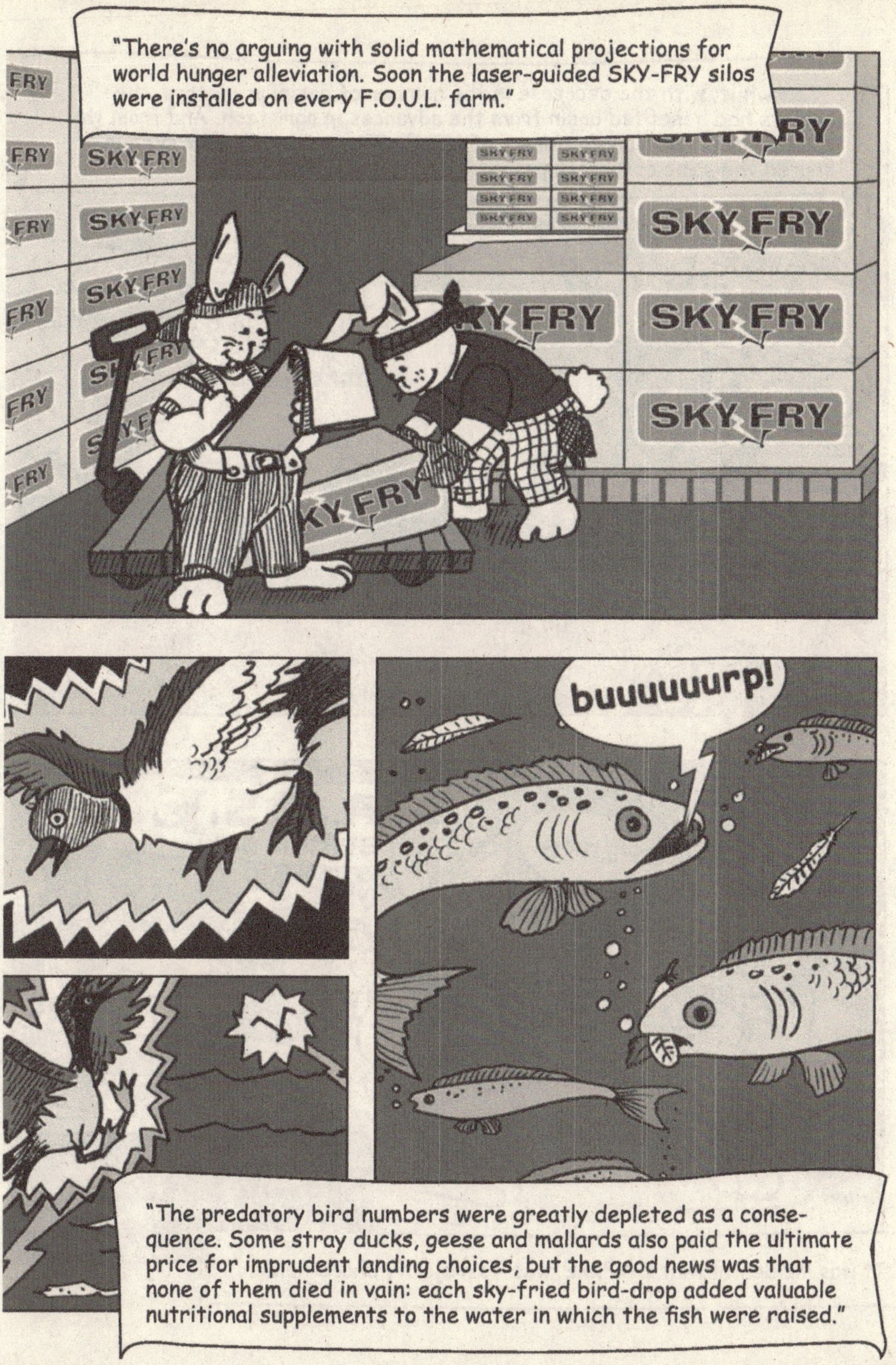

"There's no arguing with solid mathematical projections for world hunger alleviation. Soon the laser-guided SKY-FRY silos were installed on every F.O.U.L. farm."

"The predatory bird numbers were greatly depleted as a consequence. Some stray ducks, geese and mallards also paid the ultimate price for imprudent landing choices, but the good news was that none of them died in vain: each sky-fried bird-drop added valuable nutritional supplements to the water in which the fish were raised."

"Meanwhile, with the decrease in the number of aerial predators, the rabbits had benefited again from the advances in agri-tech. And from the same source: the manufacturers of UBNEXT and the SKY-FRY system shared the same corporate parent."

"It was incidental that L.A.P.S.E. was its majority share-holder."

New Fiction
Not Another
Voice

Bina Shah

The imam from the mosque in Sharon would arrive within the hour to help with the burial rites. Until Bashir came back to sign the death certificate and set all the events in motion, the baby was sleeping peacefully in the morgue.

In her hospital bed Khadija too slept, still under the effects of the anesthesia her doctor, Luisa Ramirez, had given her during surgery. The meconium was only a symptom of the real problem, the baby was born without lung tissue, Luisa conjectured, there was no point considering placental damage, a uterine prolapse, a spontaneous rupture. Malpractice was out of the question. There had been no cord accident that they could blame her for. No slowing down of movement inside the womb, no absence of kicks. There was no way to know it was going to happen—until it did.

Zainab's head was covered with a scarf; as she sat by her daughter's bedside she studied the open Quran in her hands and tried to recite the words of Surah Yasin: Undoubtedly, We shall give life to the dead and We are noting down what they have sent forward and what signs they have left behind and We have already counted every thing in a clean Book. But the Arabic letters danced on the page, turning into squiggles through the tears in her eyes.

Zainab remembered when her cousin Ali had died: eighteen to her eleven, he took her out for drives after school, bought her Cokes and packets of salted peanuts from roadside vendors. He took her all the way to Saddar, up and down Elphinstone Street, past the cinemas on M.A. Jinnah Road before the 1965 war, when Indian movies were shown without restriction and Zainab knew all the movies and their stars better than her multiplication tables and spelling.

"Have you seen *Pakeeza*? What about *Mughal-e-Azam*? Isn't Madhubala the most beautiful woman in all of India?"

Ali laughed and agreed with her, and Zainab had fallen deeply in love with him. But shortly after Ali turned nineteen, he joined the army, and was killed in the war by a bomb that exploded on his truck in the Thar desert. His bones were lost somewhere in that sand, even though the army sent back his remains in a coffin with the Pakistani flag draped on top.

The funeral was distant in Zainab's mind, she had blocked it out over the years because it was simply too hurtful to remember a world without Ali in it. Her hero, her protector was gone, and Zainab could not understand why. Everything that the adults told her felt like lies: Allah is all-Just, all-Knowing, all-Wise. Allah knows best. We cannot understand His ways. He has spared Ali from something worse. It is the will of Allah that Ali should have died when he did. He was a hero, a shaheed, a martyr. Martyrs never die.

She clapped her hands over her ears and began to scream, "I don't believe you! It's not true! Just stop talking, just stop!"

The adults around her jumped, shocked by her outburst, and she was almost satisfied. But she couldn't bring herself to say the one thing that she really wanted to, "I hate God—He took Ali away from me."

She had never watched another Indian movie again. Instead, she turned to religion, hoping every day that the prayers and recitation of the Quran would drown out the blasphemy in her heart. Now again it surfaced, like a corpse bobbing up to the surface of the water after four decades of lying on the ocean floor. It drowned out anything else in Zainab's mind as she watched her daughter lying pale and still on the hospital bed, as if she too were dead. Zainab could not help but feel the cruelty of Allah like a physical pain, as if someone had beaten her, broken every bone in her body.

She let out a long breath and began to recite, "There is no God but Allah, and Mohammed is his Messenger." Then a twin thought emerged, swimming between the words of the Kalima, she was petrified of having to be the one to tell Khadija what had happened to the baby. Zainab was not weak. She had been through a lifetime of struggle, childbirth and marriage, raising a family in a foreign land, but she was not strong enough for this.

Just as her anger at Bashir began to grow, the door opened and her son-in-law was there, stepping into the room, taking off his coat, standing in front of Zainab wordlessly. His face was pale and there were huge sunken shadows under his eyes, a few snowflakes in his hair. It was late for snowfall, but not impossible here in New England where the weather was capricious. Like God's moods, she thought to herself. Like His blessings.

Bashir stepped over to the bed and put his hand on Khadija's forehead. Zainab had to look away from the gesture, it was too full of love and anguish, too sacred to be witnessed by anyone, even her.

And then, Khadija stirred and opened her eyes.

The Alams and Khans sat in the corridor, too grief-stricken to do anything else but wait, until the imam approached them, a short middle-aged man wearing a ski jacket over a shalwar kameez, snow boots, a skullcap perched on the top of his balding head.

"I am Abdulahad Nawaaz. You are the aggrieved family?" he said to Rahim Alam, the eldest male in the gathering.

"Yes, it's my son's..."

"Inna lilla he wa inallahe rajeoon. To Allah we belong and truly, to Him we shall return," the imam said, translating into English for Katie, although Sami, Rahim's son, also looked nervous and unsure. These American-born children, so lost, the imam thought to himself. Why were they never taught the customs of Islam?

"Now, I must tell you that there is no need for janaza," Nawaaz continued, rubbing his hands together, cracking the knuckles. Qudsia, Bashir's mother, winced at the sound.

Rahim was startled. "No need for… but why… I mean, why not?"

Abbas Khan rose slowly at this pronouncement, standing shoulder to shoulder with Rahim, as they had so often stood at Friday prayers together. "Of course there must be a janaza."

Nawaaz said, "The baby was born dead, yes? So there is no need. The funeral prayer is not given for a stillbirth."

"No!" said Qudsia. "The baby was not born dead… he was alive, but then he… couldn't breathe, and suffocated." Her voice cracked on the last word.

Rahim, himself a retired doctor, was glad that the imam was there to take charge, despite his clumsy manner, his insensitivity. Things were done differently in America, death certificates, funeral homes, hearses, instead of the simple washing and shrouding done at home, the slow sad walk to the graveyard, a simple wooden cradle overlaid with roses. Rahim sometimes thought of the day when he would be in that final resting place—the aramgah, as the Sufis called it. But it was no place for a newborn child.

He put his arm around Qudsia's waist and they both sagged into each other, as if they were sharing the same thought.

The imam averted his eyes, discomfited by the contact between husband and wife. "And of course there must be no question of an autopsy. Do not let the hospital officials try to pressure you. It is strictly not allowed in Islam."

In Pakistan Rahim had often complained about families' unwillingness to allow autopsies, cadaver organ donations, anything in the name of science that would help his profession understand disease and death. But the idea of this baby's body cut open, organs removed and weighed, tissue sliced away from the heart or stomach and turned into slides for medical students to study—it was obscene.

He said, through clenched teeth, "No autopsy. Bashir won't sign the consent forms." I won't let him, he added to himself. He plunged bravely on. "Please, Imam sahib, what is your name again?"

"Abdulahad Nawaaz, brother. And you are Rahim Alam, yes?"

"I am. It's my son's… my son and daughter-in-law who have lost… we don't know what to do. Please help us, Imam sahib."

Nawaaz softened. "Where is the body?"

"In the morgue."

"I see, I see," Nawaaz murmured. "And have you called a funeral director? The washing and shrouding will take place after the baby is released to us."

"Can it not be done at home?" Qudsia whispered.

Nawaaz shook his head. "I'm sorry, it can't. Because of the health codes there are too many restrictions. But we will take care of your—" He looked questioningly at Rahim.

"It was a boy," said Rahim. "My pota."

"Paternal grandson," whispered Sami to Katie, who nodded, bewildered that this should even be a distinction.

"We will take care of him," continued Nawaaz. "We'll take care of it all. According to the proper customs. Don't worry. We must arrange for the funeral plot, so that it can be done today."

"That's too soon!" said Zainab. "I mean… Khadija isn't even awake yet… she has to be told."

"Does anyone have to travel to be here?"

"No, but…"

"I can't delay it more than forty-eight hours. It's essential that it be done as soon as possible."

"Where…" said Abbas. He seemed as though he'd aged a decade in one day, beard white, head bowed. His body had become their representative, all their grief flashed around the room like the light reflected off mirrors, until it settled on him and illuminated him in all his frailty.

"The Muslim section of the cemetery in Chelmsford."

"You'll need a coffin?" This was Katie, trying to be helpful.

Sami took Katie's hand and squeezed it hard, speaking in a low voice. "We don't use coffins."

"No, but something does need to be used for transport. The coffins come to the funeral home in wooden boxes, they will let us use one for free," explained Nawaaz. "And one so small… well, I don't think it will be a problem."

Alia, Bashir's sister, spoke up. "What are we supposed to wear?" She was unprepared for the blank look on Nawaaz's face.

"What are you supposed to wear when?"

"To the funeral," said Alia. "Should we wear black, or white, or…? Will shalwar-kameez be the right thing?"

"But you can't be thinking of coming to the funeral?" Nawaaz said.

"Why not?"

"Women can't go to graveyards."

"What?" Alia glanced at her brother. "Tell me this isn't true, Sami bhai. How can we not be allowed to go to the cemetery?"

"I don't know," mumbled Sami weakly, feeling Katie's hand slip out of his sweaty grasp. "It's a custom… in Pakistan."

"But we're not in Pakistan—we're in America!" Alia turned to Rahim in supplication. "That's why you left Pakistan, Baba, so that we wouldn't have to be slaves to stupid mullahs! You said so yourself!"

"If the imam says that you can't go, then you can't," said Rahim, burning with shame at her disrespect, the way she answered back in front of everyone. He looked to his wife for support, but Qudsia had closed her eyes and lowered her head into her hands. Rahim suddenly realised that she, too, would be excluded from the final rites for the baby. But the imams and mullahs always had the final say in matters of religion. They couldn't escape that, just because they were in America; they would always need the religious men to guide them at times like these.

At that moment, Abbas cleared his throat. The rasping sound cut through the tumult, the arguing girl, the protesting imam, Rahim trying to placate them all. They slowly fell silent, turn by turn.

"With your permission, Imam Sahib…"

Nawaaz took off his skullcap and scratched his head. "Yes, brother?"

Abbas drew himself to his full height, and suddenly he was strong-backed, magnificent. He had been an army officer of some repute, wounded in the 1971 war, before leaving the service and emigrating to America. Thirty years later, he still had the ability to command any situation, just by standing straight and casting an examining glance over the people in a room. "I would like to issue a fatwa."

Nawaaz's jaw dropped. "You want to what?"

"A fatwa," Abbas continued calmly, as if nobody had interrupted him.

"You can't…" began Nawaaz.

"A fatwa," said Abbas, for the third time, "allowing the women of my family to go to the cemetery for the burial of my nawasa. If they wish," he added, throwing a glance at Zainab, who was watching him warily.

"Are you a Shia?" said Nawaaz disdainfully. "Because we don't do this in the Sunni tradition."

"No," said Abbas pleasantly, as if he had been asked what time it was. "But as the head of my family, I allow it. They will go."

Nawaaz stared at Abbas, dumbstruck. Alia raised her face to Abbas, like a sunflower searching out the light. Qudsia nodded her head; Katie bit her lip and turned to Sami for confirmation.

Rahim staring at Abbas, incredulous that he was daring to counter the words of the imam. He had no idea if Abbas was within his rights or out of his mind, but he quickly added, "I allow my wife and daughters to go also."

Nawaaz's cheeks grew dark with indignation. "But it is not done, it is not seemly, others will not like it… the mosque… the committee…"

"Imam sahib," said Abbas, his voice still gentle. "Do you have children?"

"Why—yes."

"Mashallah. And they are all healthy and strong?"

Nawaz nodded slowly.

Abbas continued, "God is so kind, so kind. So we must show some kindness as well, isn't it true? Especially to my daughter, who has lost her child today. A grieving mother already has her place guaranteed her in Paradise, has she not?

"Then how can we not allow her to go to the kabristan, to see her first and only son properly buried? Would you want to take the responsibility of denying her that right?"

Nawaaz glared at Abbas, suddenly robbed of his authority to cast judgment on this family. Let it be on their heads, he thought crossly to himself. These mad people; no respect for the ways of Allah. Spoilt by living too many years in this Kafir land. "I will go to ring the funeral director now. Rahim bhai, please you will come with me?"

Before following the imam who was already striding powerfully down the hall, Rahim squeezed his wife's arm, trying to transfer some of his own newfound courage to her; then embraced Abbas, unsure whether to feel grateful or resentful of yet another display of dominance by his son's father-in-law.

"The imam is right. Women cannot go. It's the rule." Zainab's voice was hard and clear, her fingers clicking the beads of the tasbih that dangled from her hand in counterpoint. "Women should stay at home and mourn in private. I will not go."

Abbas bowed his head in response and began to pray.

Khadija lay in bed at the hospital, weakened and pale, while everyone else went out in the rain to bury her son. She'd begged them to wait, telling them that she would be fine in another day, to let her finish what she and Bashir had begun nine months ago.

But the doctors forbade her to leave, fearful as much for her emotional state as her physical one. And then the imam told them that too much time had passed and he could wait no longer for Khadija to recover. The funeral had to take place today.

So Bashir left her; her mother and father, too, amidst tears and prayers and promises from the nurses that they would look after her. Then finally the last nurse instructed her to rest and offered her extra pain medication, which Khadija refused, because she wanted to feel something. Agony was better than the nothingness that encased her from the neck down, her whole body a meaningless cipher.

For a while her mind was blank. Mental pictures of her family in a black hearse, a small coffin in the back, would not come, even though she tried her best to bring them up. But their faces were blurry; the black car kept turning into their blue Volvo; the coffin refused to take shape or color.

Her fingers began to move across her body, up to her breasts, still full with the hormones of pregnancy. Khadija had watched them grow since last summer, her normally flat, boyish chest suddenly taking on a life of its own, ballooning to cartoonish proportions almost overnight. Her nipples had become as dark and as big as black plates, and they were constantly sore; mysterious green veins appeared like seaweed beneath the pale swell of her breasts.

"I hate having these—these watermelons!" she'd hissed out of nowhere one evening, clutching them in her hands and shaking them in disgust.

Bashir was in bed next to her, reading a crime novel. He looked up, startled, then doubled over and laughed and laughed until he cried, then choked on his own tears. His glasses fell off his nose when Khadija punched him in the arm.

"It's not funny," she shouted. "You try carrying these goddamn things everywhere, see how you like it when men don't look at your eyes anymore, just have conversations with your chest!"

Bashir leaned over and addressed her breasts, "That's terrible!" Khadija grabbed the paperback and whacked him with it, leading to twenty minutes of raucous passion that left them both surprised, sweaty and gasping when it was over. They lay back, separated in the darkness, and when Khadija felt the baby kick inside her, she marvelled that for these few months of her life, she would never be alone.

And now for the first time, there was nobody else but her in the room.

Khadija's hands moved down to her stomach. It was not flat, but deflated, the skin hanging in strange creases over her belly, swollen and heavy. She fingered the bandages over the incision, a long vertical cut that travelled from navel to pubis. The scar would look like a long zipper when it had healed and faded.

The nausea hit her like a kick to the stomach, the retching so violent that she thought she might pass out. She thought she could feel blood at the back of her throat, but that was impossible. It was her stomach she had bled from, and her vagina—the discharge after childbirth, thin and watery, but a sign that her body still had no idea things were not normal at all.

Ruby, the nurse, came hurrying in. "What's the matter, darling, are you vomiting again? Here, use this..." She passed a kidney-shaped steel bowl to Khadija, who took it in her shaky grasp and heaved, but nothing came up.

Khadija handed the bowl back to Ruby with a weak laugh, trying to avoid tangling the IV line in her vein. "I didn't know I'd vomited before… hope I didn't make too much of a mess."

"You did, a little. It was no problem. Then you went back to sleep."

"I don't remember."

"It's the anesthesia… it can… Oh my, what's happened here?"

Her voice was mild, the Southern accent genteel, not obtrusive, but Khadija found it grating. "I don't know," muttered Khadija.

Ruby's soft hands were lifting up her nightgown, and then she clicked her tongue. "You strained your stitches." She turned around and left the room.

Khadija lay there, resentful and frightened; she expected Luisa to come back in Ruby's wake, to warn against the damage Khadija could have done to her neat stitches, scold her like an angry bird and write a prescription for some strong anti-depressants. But a few moments later, Ruby returned with fresh bandages. She deftly cleaned off the small drops of blood that had sprung out and around the stitches, then proceeded to reapply the bandages to Khadija's abdomen, her sweet face screwed up all the while in a frown of concentration that reminded Khadija of a small child puzzling over a difficult question in math class.

"Call me if you need anything," she said when she was done. Khadija turned her face away and stared at the wall, not caring whether Ruby stayed or left. Lost in the flow of her own thoughts, she didn't notice when Ruby padded away again.

They would all be at the funeral home right now. Khadija had whispered frantically to Bashir that she didn't want the imam to touch the baby, and Bashir nodded, bewildered by her vehemence and the sudden responsibility thrust upon him. With no time or inclination for prayers or the Quran, not fasting during Ramadan, blissfully unmoved by his mother's exhortations to become more religious, Bashir would be as useless as an atheist at his own child's funeral.

But Khadija didn't care who washed the baby, man or woman, as long as it wasn't Nawaaz. She imagined Bashir, directed by the imam, unfolding their child's limbs as if he were unwrapping a present, and rubbing them with rosewater. Her mother would place cotton in its tiny mouth and nose, tying the jaw with a small white cloth so it wouldn't flop open. Who had brought the piece of unstitched cloth for the funeral shroud? What prayers would be said over the grave?

Khadija clenched her fists in frustration. If only she could leap out of the bed and walk downstairs, hail a cab, go to the funeral home to make sure that they were taking care with the baby, being gentle with his delicate skin, his fine hair.

She tried, experimentally, to swing her feet round to the edge of the bed and push herself off, but there was no strength in her legs. Her whole body was too heavy to move, she was going nowhere for now. She didn't want to risk an infection. Luisa would not allow it.

Luisa had entered the room soon after Khadija woke up from the anesthesia, Bashir sitting next to her, holding her hand as if she would disappear if he let her go. Her mother wanted to be there too, but Bashir insisted that it be only the two of them when Khadija was told what had happened. Zainab retreated tearfully to the hallway, where she sat with Qudsia on the hard blue plastic chairs, the two women side by side, companions in frozen despair.

Luisa sat down on the other side of the bed and took Khadija's hand.

"Khadija, I have something to tell you."

Khadija's heart, still influenced by the cocktail of drugs running through her body, continued to beat steadily as Luisa told Khadija that the baby had not survived. "We did everything, but it wasn't good enough. The meconium pointed to a bigger problem, an abnormality in the lungs. There was a one in a million chance of this happening. We were that one in a million." She paused, then looked down at Khadija's hand enclosed in her own. "Please forgive me."

Khadija stared at Luisa's mouth as it formed sounds that made no sense to her. Any moment she knew Luisa would say, "Sorry, it's a mistake. Your baby is fine, he's waiting to see you." But it never happened. She wanted to jerk her hand out of Luisa's grasp, but she could not move.

Bashir stroked her cheek and her hair and bent to her ear, his lips pressed against it, whispering, I'm sorry, I'm so, so sorry. His tears were wetting her hair and she tried to lift her hand to brush them away—they were seeping into her skin, trickling like ants on her scalp. She had waited for this moment far longer than nine months; she had been waiting all her life, ever since she had met Bashir and known that she wanted to have his children. The certainty took her by surprise, so clear and strong, like sexual desire, only more pronounced and sharp-edged than lust. Nobody could cheat her of this moment, or of the lifetime ahead that she had built in her head, anticipating her own birth on the day her child was born.

She strained to lift her arms. Bashir sensed the movement and began to rub them as they lay like dead limbs at her sides. Then she half-closed her eyes, and made both Luisa and Bashir disappear. She was aware of more people floating in and out of the room, her mother, her father, Bashir's mother. There was only one person Khadija wanted to see, who never came.

Time and space ceased to exist. Comfort beckoned from the void that only sleep could give. Khadija sank into it gratefully, feeling it erase everything from her consciousness, feeling everything falling away from her.

Then new hands were shaking her awake. "Khadija, it's time."

Khadija turned sleepily and peeked out from beneath her eyelids. Luisa was bent over her bed, her normally fresh skin pale and patchy, her blue eyes tired. "Khadija, we thought you'd want to hold the baby." She reached out to grasp Khadija's shoulders and hold them while Khadija struggled awake, pushing up with difficulty, a groan escaping her lips.

She saw Bashir near the door, holding a little bundle. She thought her heart might stop at that moment. All her previous desire to hold the baby in her arms suddenly died.

"Luisa… what?" she slurred, her tongue feeling heavy in her mouth. "No… I don't want to…"

Bashir stepped forward hesitantly. "The imam wants the funeral to take place today, Khadija. I told him you weren't well enough but he doesn't want to wait any longer."

"No… he has to…"

"You should see the baby, Khadija. You'll regret it if you don't." Luisa spoke with certainty.

"But…" Khadija looked beseechingly at her husband, who misunderstood the glance and handed the bundle to Luisa, dazed, as if he too had been wakened suddenly from a deep sleep.

Luisa took it tenderly and moved the blanket away from the baby's face. "Here, Khadija," she said. "Hold him."

Khadija didn't know where to look. She glanced at Bashir, who bit his lip like a small child; at Luisa, who had walked to the window to give them the privacy that the small room could not afford; at the darkening shadows cast on the walls by the sun going behind clouds.

When her eyes flickered down towards the bundle in her arms, her mind doubled with confusion. He was alive, peacefully asleep; his eyes were closed, but he was breathing, his chest moving up and down like a swallow's.

Khadija put out her finger and stroked the hair on his forehead, smoothing it down. Then she traced his nose and chin, brought her fingertip to his cheeks, felt the outline of his lips. She touched his skin and imagined that it was warm, not cool, that it was not pale, but flushed rosy red with new blood.

Bashir and Luisa watched her closely, looking for signs of shock. When she began to shake, they grew alarmed, and when her tears fell onto the baby's face, they came to take him away from her. She wanted to fight them, to scream, to demand that they let her be with her child. But she said nothing, just hunched down over the baby protectively and trembled.

Bashir reached gently into her arms and drew out the baby. Luisa stretched out her hands to receive it from him, but Bashir shook his head, casting one last look at Khadija. Luisa walked out of the room, and then Bashir followed her through the open door.

Khadija watched her entire world leave in Bashir's arms. She crumpled into the bed and disappeared inside herself again.

He came back, hours later, when it was night and she was fully awake, lying in the darkness and counting the cracks in the wall. She recognised his black suit from their wedding reception—he'd been able to keep it, not putting on any weight since the day they'd gotten married.

He sat down on the edge of the bed and searched for her face in the darkness. After a moment, he sighed and lay down beside her. She shifted slightly to make room for him, moaning, even small movements were starting to hurt now. He felt alien, a stranger in her bed.

After an age, he whispered, "Do you want to know what happened?"

She shook her head. "No more talking," she said. She was empty, concave, and nobody in the world could understand how it felt to be a waning moon when she should have been feeling like Mother Earth.

He put his arm around her shoulder, awkwardly, hugging her to him. She stiffened, feeling the cold on his damp jacket. She could smell the leaves, the grass, the outdoor air laced with the minty tinge of pine trees. She could smell the scent of her child on his shirt.

New Nonfiction
The Last Moghul of Shalimar

Ahmad Rafay Alam

The Shalimar Garden lies about five miles east of the Walled City of Lahore. If one still travelled by bullock-cart, it's about a half day's ride from the city and just about the place you would want to stop and rest if you were travelling there on the Grand Trunk Road.

There's another garden rest-stop north-east of the city as well, in Shahdara, on the other side of the river Ravi. The Moghul Emperor Jehangir's remains are buried here. Sort of. Quite the alcoholic, Jehangir had developed a cold his immune system couldn't quite shake off. He was vacationing in Kashmir, and it was advised that, for his health, he be brought down to warmer Lahore. He died on the road on the way back and, just to make things complicated, his last words, "Kashmir, only Kashmir", meant that a practical compromise had to be reached. He was eviscerated and his innards dispatched to Kashmir and his skin and bones, so to speak, were carried forth and buried in Lahore in an estate that belonged to his widow, the formidable Nur Jehan.

Nur Jehan also ensured that her father, the Emperor's Prime Minister Asif Jah, be buried nearby and, later, when she passed away in 1645, she directed that she be interred in a "simple" grave overlooking the tombs of the Men in Her Life. Of course, nothing built of white marble in 1645 is "simple", though the grave is designed not to draw attention to itself, unlike the structures it overlooks. This is signature Nur Jehan, considered to have been the real power behind the Peacock Throne.

Although the first Islamic garden in South Asia wasn't built by a Moghul (it was built by the dynasty they overthrew), it was these descendants of Tamerlane—"Moghul" was the word to describe a Mongol who had converted to Islam—who perfected the form. The Moghul garden is quite a thing to behold. Aside from being stunningly beautiful, it is a manifestation of power and ego unequalled in the world.

Aware that the founder of the dynasty had died in Kabul and that the second Moghul Emperor had spent most of his reign in exile, it was the third Moghul, the Great Emperor Akbar, who saw to it that his father's burial site made an unequivocal political statement: that the Moghul was not a marauding nomad; that the Moghul was there to stay and had chosen the soil of Hindustan as his eternal resting place. Then, in the great Persian and Islamic horticultural traditions, Akbar went about ensuring the gardens surrounding Humayun's tomb resembled paradise.

The word paradise comes from the Persian phrase for "surrounded by a wall". From the Semitic concept of Eden, where from a well water flows in four directions, we get the idea of the *charbagh* surrounded by a wall encompassing Eden and keeping it from the outside world. Putting Humayun's grave in the middle of the *charbagh* was another unequivocal statement:

that from this resting place of the Great Moghul springs forth a garden of paradise. The Moghuls, you must understand, were not circumspect about these things. And a Moghul garden, like I said, is quite a thing to behold.

According to legend, one night as he slept in the garden near his father Jehangir's final resting place, the Moghul Emperor Shah Jehan (he of the Taj Mahal) dreamt of a garden more beautiful than the ones built by Jehangir in temperate Kashmir. The Moghuls detested the weather in the Indus plains, repeatedly cribbed about it and constantly yearned, like anyone flung into diaspora, for the perfection that was back home. In their case, back home was Samarkand and Afghanistan, their invigorating weather and pleasurable fruits. When the Emperor awoke, he summoned two of his more prominent courtiers, and ordered them to construct for him a garden more beautiful than any other. This was in the early 1640s, and it is how the Shalimar Garden eventually came to be.

One of the courtiers summoned by the Emperor was said to be Ali Mardan Khan. By all accounts an ambitious political survivor, Khan had finagled his way into the governorship of Lahore and Kashmir. And just a few years before Shah Jehan dreamt of the Shalimar Garden, Khan had casually let it be known that there was an engineer in his employ who had the ability to construct a great canal that would bring water to the parched lands around Lahore.

The Walled City of Lahore lies at a high point along the Ravi flood plain. Although the river flowed north of the city, it was unwieldy and known to flood nearby low-lying areas. This meant that although the city had drinking water, it was impossible to use the river to irrigate much of the nearby land. This, in turn, meant that the city relied for its food on grain and goods brought through the Grand Trunk Road and whatever harvests the monsoons yielded. With a perennial canal, however, all that could change. Food would be available in abundance throughout the year and political stability not too far behind.

And so the Shah Nehr, the Emperor's Canal, was built. And it was built in that remarkable fashion that only the whimsy of kings can provoke. From over 170 kilometers away, where the Ravi leaves the mountains and joins the plains of the Punjab, the canal was dug so that the water level would remain, at all times, higher than the level needed at Shalimar. Mind you, this is still the 1640s we're talking about. This was no easy task. Ali Mardan Khan took over Rs. 100,000 for this task, an astronomical amount in the day. And there's something reassuring in the fact that, the more things change, the more they stay the same. Khan's engineer turned out to be no match for the task. Another engineer had to be engaged to complete it. Khan managed to extricate himself in the way that only the privileged can escape liability.

The Shah Nehr was completed over-budget and years after its original deadline. But it did what it was supposed to: it irrigated the Shalimar Gardens. At the time, this was also a gratuitous display of the Emperor's power over nature. Here he could dream and, lo! The next day nature would yield to his command. Arid land became verdant, exotic plants blossomed and large trees could grow under the shade of the Great Moghul's peace.

The Garden itself is laid out in three levels. The water enters the Garden from the south through the upper terrace, called the *Farah Baksh* or bestower of pleasures. This is where the harem was, and getting caught there without good reason was a capital offence. From the first terrace to the second, the water cascaded down a wall of precious gems and stones and then under the Peacock Throne itself before flowing into a large pool. This is where the Emperor received guests and held court. The third and lowest level, the *Hayat Baksh*, the bestower of life, received water flowing from the central pool to the *Sawan Bhawan*, a sunken tank with niches on three walls where, until the 1960s the great *Mela Chiraghan* celebrating the Sufi mysticism of Madhu Lal Shah Hussain took place. From there the water flows to the north of the Garden to the Emperor's own chamber, or *serai*. From the *serai*, the Emperor could look up onto *Sawan Bhawan*, the cascade and the fountains, the innumerable trees, plants, flowers and, of course the harem. From this vantage point, even today, once the magnificence of the Garden sinks in, a certain sense of envy hits visitors: It must have been good to be the king.

The water from Shah Nehr then went to irrigate nearby land, which belonged to the Mian family. In fact, the Mians must have been in quite a quandary when Shah Jehan approached them with his idea for a pleasure garden. The proposed site was right on their land, and court protocol must have dictated that it be handed over as a gift to please the Emperor's fancy. But they were rewarded. The Mians were appointed the custodians of the Garden. I suppose this gave them some access to Shah Jehan himself, and thus a small stake in local politics. In any event, the water from the Shah Nehr helped develop what was left of their holding into a verdant suburb, Baghbanpura, the village of gardens, one of Lahore's first suburbs.

Baghbanpura is also where the shrine of Madhu Lal Shah Hussain is located. The uninitiated may be forgiven for thinking this is just the shrine of a Sufi mystic. But the story of the Sufi ascetic Shah Hussain and his much younger Brahman disciple, Madhu, is perhaps the most colourful tale of homosexual love in the history of these parts.

Shah Hussain, in the great tradition of Sufi saints, was an iconoclast. By shunning the pleasures and obligations of the world, he made himself independent of whatever local political affiliation one needed to keep up with the Joneses in rural India. His point of departure was a verse he came across that told him "The life of this world is nothing but a game and sport" and this was the pivot on which he rejected the status quo of society and the political structure of Moghul India. It may even have been the reason why he so scandalously took up with Madhu, a Hindu boy nearly half his age. Tales of Shah Hussain's infatuation with Madhu, whom he first set eyes on in a crowded Lahori bazaar, are legendary. One of the miracles attributed to him is how he blinded a group of Madhu's relatives who, having caught the couple *in flagrante delicto*, attempted to "honour kill" them.

Nevertheless, the great love and friendship between the two is the source of many of Shah Hussain's many *kafis*. Madhu took up his mentor's role after Shah Hussain's death and, forty eight years later, was buried right next to him in the Baghbanpura graveyard.

Every year, when the Punjab celebrates spring, hundreds of thousands of devotees flock to the shrine to take part in the *Mela Chiraghan*, the great festival of lights. In the current Islamic Republic, the Hindu iconography in the *dhamal*—there's even something close to fire worship—is testament to how Sufism, the religion of the soil of this part of the world, still represents a challenge to the status quo.

Even though Shah Hussain had, for whatever reason, taken a stance against Moghul rule, the inner strength of his message saw his status grow. By the end of the Moghul dynasty, even though he was several hundred years dead, the *Mela Chiraghan* took place inside the Shalimar Gardens. Ranjit Singh, the Sikh ruler who established control over Lahore and the Punjab in the early 1800s, used the Garden as a stable (he preferred relaxing in the baradari he'd set up between the Lahore Fort and Badshahi Masjid); a sort of last laugh at the previous rulers of the city and province he now governed. He even plundered the jewels of the cascade in the Garden. However, he let the Mians continue to maintain the Shalimar and the Sufis to continue their *Mela Chiraghan* lest he rock the boat too much. The same is true of the British, who acquired the Punjab more or less by purchase about halfway into the 19th Century. They used the Garden, among other things, as a honeymoon destination but still let the *Mela* take place even though their attitude towards "the Native" was scarcely above contempt.

After Colonial rule came the Partition and the Gardens became part of a Pakistani Lahore. In the 1960s, because of his animosity towards the stinging editorials of newspapers owned by one of the Mians of Baghbanpura, the military dictator and president at the time, Field Marshal Ayub Khan, "acquired" the Garden. Thus came to an end the faithful discharge of their obligations by the Mians who had seen the Gardens through dynasties, regime changes and Partition. The *Mela 'Chiraghan* owed its location to the continuity they provided. But with the Pakistani state's exercise of eminent domain, the Garden now belonged to the state and fell under the supervision of the Archaeology Department. The *Mela* had to relocate to the Baghbanpura graveyard where Madhu Lal and Shah Hussain rest in peace.

Since the dislocation from the Garden and especially after the Islamisation introduced by a later military dictator and president, General Zia ul Haq, the state's relationship with the *Mela* has diminished. It's difficult in Pakistan at this moment to maintain the image of a pious, hardworking government if money is being spent in the memory of a gay *pir*. But in a place like the Punjab, where the oral tradition still prevails, nothing communicates a social and political message like good poetry and the devotion of a disciple. At the moment, Governors and Chief Ministers like to appear washing the sarcophagus of "the patron Saint of Lahore", Hazrat Data Ganj Baksh Hajvery. Data Sahib's politically acceptable sexual orientation recently saw the government spend a quarter of a billion rupees on renovating his shrine.

Ghulam Murtaza is a shopkeeper. The gate to his three-storied house overlooks the road next to the back wall of the Shalimar Garden where someone has sprayed a message informing all and sundry that litter is caused by "sonsofbitches". He has to see it every day when he leaves work, which isn't too far away, just a short ways up a couple side-streets. Baghbanpura is no longer the village of gardens. Lahore's population has grown 400 percent since Partition and the city has sprawled around most of its historical monuments. Baghbanpura today is crowded, noisy and littered. Apart from what is protected by the walls of Shalimar Garden, there are no trees in Baghbanpura. Just dust, plastic bags and poles carrying electricity and phone wires.

Ghulam Murtaza usually gets driven to work on one of his sons' motorcycles. On his way, he has to pass the remains of one of the water regulation systems designed by Shah Jehan's engineers to ensure that the water to the 410 fountains in the Gardens flowed at exactly the same rate. The techniques and technology used by the Moghuls to achieve this hydrologic feat are still a mystery and many an expert has tried and failed to understand the system. In the 1990s, when the Government of Punjab thought that India-Pakistan trade might still have a chance, they decided to widen the Grand Trunk Road so that it could handle the tens of thousands of trucks and lorries they hoped would pass by. In the process, they destroyed the water regulation system. This was the reason why UNESCO now lists the Shalimar Gardens as World Heritage in Danger. Of course, now no one will learn how the Moghuls did it.

Ghulam Murtaza grew up in Baghbanpura and has lived there for the past twenty five years. He's married with two sons and a daughter, all in their teens. Though no more than five foot five, he carries himself with a swagger that only Lahoris from the Walled City or its oldest suburb can pull off. He can remember, as a child, attending the *Mela Chiraghan* along with his father back when the *Mela* still took place in the Shalimar Gardens. Now, with the *Mela* held at the Madhu Lal Shah Hussain shrine in the Baghbanpura graveyard, he says he doesn't go anymore because it's too crowded.

Ghulam Murtaza's house is located exactly behind the Emperor's *serai* on the third level of the Shalimar Gardens. Just behind the place where you can stand, look at the Gardens framing your view, and just for a minute imagine the many histories that wind themselves into its own. From the roof on the third floor of the rather basic brick-and-cement construction, Ghulam Murtaza, the last Moghul of Shalimar, has the same view Shah Jehan dreamt of. He says it isn't very good.

Contributors

Attiq Uddin Ahmed is an architect and urban designer and a freelance journalist and photographer whose work has also been published in *Absolutely Public – Crossover: Art and Architecture* (2005). He is currently working on a book titled *Surrealistan: Heroic Adventures in Architecture in Pakistan*.

Mehreen Ajaz is a sponsorship officer at ActionAid in Islamabad. She read English Literature at the University of Maryland. "Baby" is her first published work.

Ahmad Rafay Alam is an environmental lawyer based in Lahore. He is on the faculty of the Lahore University of Management Sciences and Punjab University and is a columnist for *The News* and *The Express Tribune* on environment and urban planning issues.

Sarwat Yasmeen Azeem studied English Literature and Journalism in the UK. She is a creative manager at a major advertising agency in Pakistan and hopes to have her first full-length book published soon.

Sabiha Bano prefers to remain a man/woman of mystery.

Rayika Choudri is a published short story writer and freelances in commercials and film production. She is based in Karachi.

Michelle Farooqi is an illustrator, cartoonist and book-designer. She paints in the 18th-century classical realist tradition. She is currently illustrating the children's edition of *Hoshruba*, and collaborating on the graphic novel *Rabbit Rap*. **Musharraf Ali Farooqi** is the author, among other works, of the novel *The Story of a Widow* (2008), the critically acclaimed translations of Urdu classics, *The Adventures of Amir Hamza* (2007) and the first book of a projected 24-volume magical fantasy epic, *Hoshruba* (2009). He has just finished the graphic novel *Rabbit Rap* and is currently working on a fiction collection.

Sadaf Halai has been published in *Voices and Visions: Young Writers from Pakistan* (2009) among other publications. She has poems forthcoming in the *Journal of Postcolonial Writing*. Sadaf lives in Toronto.

Mohsin Hamid is the author of the novels *Moth Smoke* (2000) and the Man Booker-shortlisted *The Reluctant Fundamentalist* (2007). He lives between Lahore, New York and London.

Mohammed Hanif is a writer and journalist. His first novel *A Case of Exploding Mangoes* (2008) was nominated for the Man Booker Prize.

Danish Islam is training as a doctor at the University College of Medicine and Dentistry, Lahore. This is his first published short story.

Madiha Sattar is Senior Assistant Editor at the monthly newsmagazine *The Herald*, where she covers Pakistani politics and culture. Her work has appeared in the Huffington Post and the AfPak Channel.

Bina Shah is the Karachi-based author of six novels and short story collections. Her writing has appeared in Pakistani publications along with the *Guardian*, the *Hindustan Times*, and in *Granta's* Online Only.

Aziz A. Sheikh is an Islamabad-based doctor. He moonlights as a columnist at *The Express Tribune* and has previously published fiction in Canada.

Bilal Tanweer's translation of Urdu pulp fiction, *The House of Fear* by Ibn-e-Safi, was published by Random House India (2010). His other translated works have appeared in *Words Without Borders*, *The Annual of Urdu Studies* and *Duniyazad*. He teaches Creative Writing at the Lahore University of Management Sciences and is currently working on a collection of short stories.